Sand, Smoke, Current

Robert Vander Lugt

Wiseblood Books

Milwaukee, Wisconsin

Copyright © 2014 by Wiseblood Books
Wiseblood Books
www.wisebloodbooks.com

Printed in the United States of America
Set in Arabic Typesetting

Dedication quote from "Insomnia" originally published in Kenyon, Jane. *Let Evening Come.* Graywolf Press: Minneapolis, MN, 1990.

"If I Had a Hammer" was included in a anthology titled *Show Off,* copyright 2012 by The Write Practice.

An earlier version of "Sand, Smoke, Current," appeared at www.thewritepractice.com

Library of Congress Cataloging-in-Publication Data
Vander Lugt, Robert, 1961-
Sand, Smoke, Current/ Robert Vander Lugt;
1. Vander Lugt, Robert, 1961—fiction

ISBN-13: 978-0615893259
ISBN-10: 0615893252

The light moves unsteadily, like someone,
whose balance is uncertain after traveling
many hours, coming a long way.
Get up. Get up and let it out.
—"Insomnia," by Jane Kenyon.

To my parents, Tunis and Ethel Vander Lugt, who
taught me about belonging, in body and soul, in life
and death.

For Vicki, from the very first story you always said yes.

TABLE OF CONTENTS

Onslaught

The storm woke, massed and then slipped over the frozen lake. Clouds, hunched and rolled like a fighter's shoulders, leaned and sparred across the star-pricked sky. At the beach they stalled, swept over low dunes. Hissing, they infiltrated the steep wooded hills guarding the shore. It spilled east, gathering speed, racing through the stubbled, sleeping cornfields with maniac delight, a thousand hollow stalks quaking like toneless wind chimes. Winter-stiff trees lined the fields, blacker-than-night sentries latticing the sky. It slammed against their skeletal frames and they rose up, groaning and twisting, frozen fibers cracking like old man bones. Their defense held no weight. The storm grabbed fistfuls of dead leaves, tossing them about like a rampaging child. Then, grasping the trees themselves, it twisted hard maple fingers in a torturer's grip. Up and down the ribbon of woods, branches popped and cracked and shrieked. Limbs gave way, the trees saved by their rending. Then it began to snow.

He dozed, waiting, the dependable old house a fortress stalwart and dark. Outside, the barnyard light seeped through the windows, faint and yellowed. Earlier, he had watched the afternoon news, nodding as the young woman pranced in front of a map so brilliantly colored that he squinted against it. Then, rubbing his knees, he had glanced at the clock and stood to his tasks. He filled the tea kettle and the coffee maker and rummaged deep in cupboards, his rattled explorations ringing pan against

1

bowl, hollow and dissonant. Dragging out a large pot, he lowered it into the sink, swung the faucet in place and watched, turning the tap off when the water threatened to overflow. He made no attempt to lift it. Instead he leaned there, gathering his breath, watching the rippled water settle flat and smooth like puddled mercury. He drew another bucket and placed it by the toilet for flushing. Returning through the hall empty-handed, he stopped and nudged the thermostat higher, then retrieved firewood from the garage, stacking it beside the stove. He tested flashlights and unwrapped candles, then stood and surveyed his preparations. *As nervous as an old woman,* he thought. With the next breath, he apologized.

The phone rang hours later, after he had dragged his chair around to face west and wrapped his legs in an old quilt against the draft. He shook his head. She did not need to call and warn him. Even before the news he'd felt the storm, not in prognosticating ill-tempered joints — his ruined hips ached without regard of the weather — but from some other sense, a crinkling of the air, a sharpening, that set his mind anxious. He let the phone buzz. It stopped, sat idle, and then rang again.

"Hello." he rasped.

"Dad. It's Tess. How are things up there?"

"Just fine, 'cept the power's out and the drifts are over the barn and I'll probably run out of provisions before the sled dogs break through."

"Funny, Dad. I've been watching the weather. It's supposed to be a bad one."

"Every last one is supposed to be a bad one. I'm fine. It's winter, it's just doing what it's supposed to do. I'm set if the power goes out. Plenty of wood, water's drawn.

2

Candles and flashlights galore. If you lived any closer, I'd invite ya over for popcorn."

"I wish I did, Dad. I'd come if I could. I called Chad. He'll check on you tomorrow."

"Chad. Good kid. And I'd like a visit, but the roads could get bad. You know how it drifts out here. Let him stay put, 'less I call him."

"How's your breathing? Your blood pressure?"

"All fine, and yes, I'm using my cane." His eyes searched out its location.

"Really?"

"Most of the time. Believe me, I'm terrified you'll find out I'm misbehaving or something and pack me down to Indianapolis."

"It's not such a bad place, you know."

"Fine place, but not for me. Not yet. There's an order to things. First gotta do the condo and the apartment and the assisted living thing. Then, when I'm a drooling, wheel-chaired, numb-minded and diapered old goat, I'll let ya drag me down there. See then if you still want me."

"Dad! Of course I'd want you. I'd show you off to my friends. A few of them think crotchety old men in wheelchairs are cute."

"Don't worry, no child of mine is changing my diaper or wiping my butt. If that time comes, I'll find some nice nursing home full of potted plants and pretty nurses and settle in. But don't think it'll be tomorrow."

"Course not, Daddy. That'll probably never happen. I just hate that you're all alone."

"Lonely. Sometimes." He corrected, "Never completely alone. I do miss you, though. You're a good daughter for

3

calling. Now get off the phone so you can keep an eye on the weather for me."

"Love you, Dad."

"Love you."

He replaced the phone and sank into the chair, the silence settling with his old bones. His fingers dropped on the worn upholstery, spindled and knobby. He hated the look of them, skeletons of stronger memories. Outside, the black night danced with snow, smothering the tea-stain of light leaking from the barnyard pole. Past the barn a trio of spruces swayed, jagged teeth bared against the storm, and he imagined the smell of them as the wind raked their black needles. Frigid air wheezed through the window frame.

He closed his eyes, thought of the fields beyond the trees, their corduroy rows frozen rocklike, bristled with the remnants of harvest. The acres were no longer his, first leased and finally sold off to the big Lutheran boy down the road. The land contract stipulated that the land would grow crops, not sub-divisions, for at least ten years. That first October after the sale, he'd sat here stronger and watched the harvest, dust chasing the machines, shrouding their sharp edges. It drifted high, a lace filter for the setting sun, and he knew some would fall unnoticed on his property, talc his windows grey. He'd chuckled and counted it a veiled blessing, a portion of his old fields returned to him.

He slept again. The wind whined, buffeting the house and sucking the window sash in and out. Somewhere a power line snapped and darkness fell hard with it. A gust burst down the flue and tossed sparks in the woodstove. He started, suddenly awake, and rose to light candles and retrieve the tea kettle from the kitchen. He set it on the woodstove and returned to the chair. The kettle warmed slowly and he was sleeping again when it finally whistled shrill in the storm-rattled room. It did not wake him. His sleep was filled with dark dreams of windswept lands, ashen and debris-tossed, hollow houses stripped of shingles and siding, frameworks bent under forces shrieking and unseen.

Later, he woke, poured a cup of hot water and stood steeping his tea at the window. Snow flew horizontal, flattening against the pane in wet globs, melting and running in snaking trails that merged and funneled mindlessly. He saw nothing beyond the glass; the barn, the squat equipment shed, the dancing evergreens all obliterated. Instead, he appraised his reflection, a hunched old man with cavern cheeks, hair sparse and wisped, his whole frame stripped. The face stared back expectant, neither fearless nor frightened. He rubbed his stubble, wondered when he'd last shaved and resolved to do it in the morning. *I am getting lazy*, he thought.

Past midnight the north-south roads stacked with drifts, the snow building against fence lines and road cuts and the slightest rise in landscape. The county crews abandoned the criss-cross of country roads. Instead, trucks teamed in pairs to plow the highways and major arteries, hoping to keep one lane traversable. The prudent stayed home, while the foolish— inexperienced young, drunks and the importantly invincible—staggered forth, their confidence locked in four wheel drive. Some grasped reality and gave up. Others, desperate or delusional, slid in to ditches and buried themselves in drifts. The storm, having neither sought nor pursued them, swallowed all without notice.

An old pale green Toyota turned down the road, slowed, and then plunged forward, busting two drifts before veering right and skating into the ditch. The driver had stubbornly shrugged off his parents' warnings. His first few miles were fearless, his recklessness disguised as skill. He drove with one hand on the wheel, the other on her thigh, tapping both to the songs on the radio. She had sat silent and supportive beside him, but her confidence dimmed in the swirling snow. Then they argued. First over the route. She was sure the interstate was safest; he was convinced they'd make better time using country roads. She knew they were lost before he did, or at least before he admitted it. Maybe he was trying to make them late; he had never wanted to go to the party in the first place.

Now, hopelessly ditch bound, they argued again. He insisted on going alone, leaving her warm in the buried car. She did not want to stay behind, both for her own sake and for his. She worried they would find him days later, smothered in the snow. The house they both spotted earlier came into view so infrequently she began to doubt its existence.

"No, damn it. You're staying." He slammed his fist in the steering wheel. The wipers swept back and forth, carving icy arcs out of the storm.

"Go!" she hissed, "But I will not sit here alone forever. I'll come after you."

"No. You're not dressed for it. You'll freeze. I can do this." He gripped the wheel with both hands and stared ahead. "I swear I saw a house or something. You said you saw it, too. It's not that far. Please don't leave the car.

Promise?" Finally, she nodded, but her lips remained a taut, defiant line.

He pushed hard against the door, driving it repeatedly against the snow until he could squeeze clear. Snow poured in behind him. He needed to kick it away with his sneakered feet before he could slam the door shut. He sank waist deep with his next step, sprawling face first, arms not long enough to break his fall. Scrambling up, he wiped his face with a snow-covered sleeve and turned back to the car. The dash lights washed her face a pale, anxious blue. Then he turned into the wind and waded down the road.

He followed the road blindly, crossing to the opposite side when it felt right. He fell again at the opposite ditch, but, prepared this time, stood immediately, bolstered by his progress. The snow drove so hard he nearly walked into a tree, and he stopped and sheltered behind its massive trunk. Then, pushing into the wind again, he saw the house, a grey shadow buttressed against the storm. He jolted forward, falling once or twice until the snow lessened behind the house and he skidded up the steps. He pounded the door with his sleeve-clenched fist.

The old man woke and listened. Then he stood and shuffled, bewildered, to the never-used front door. There was no light to switch on, no way to see the other side, so he just swung the door in. The boy, whispering shivered thanks, pushed past him. The old man closed the door and they stared at each other for a moment, the boy stomping and brushing snow off until the man waved him to the woodstove.

He dragged a kitchen chair to the stove and commanded the boy to sit, pulled the quilts from his chair, and draped the boy's convulsing shoulders. He poured hot water into a cup for tea and handed it to the

7

boy, listening as he shivered, his frozen words making little sense to the old man's sleep-dulled ears. He waited, propped on the arm of his chair. After the first few sips of tea, the boy's lips regained color and the ability to form speech.

"We're stuck."

"We?" It took a few seconds for the plural pronoun to register. "Who is 'we'?"

"My girlfriend. She's in the car."

"In the car! You left her in the car? Is it running?" He stood without waiting for an answer and left the room. The boy watched him go.

"I think so, to keep her warm, was that bad?"

He listened to the faint scraping of drawers.

The man returned dressed in the plaid woolen reds of a hunter. He tossed a pile on the boy's lap—worn waffle underwear, a flannel shirt, a pair of dark blue work pants that would not fit.

"Get dressed." He said and left the room again.

The boy stripped in front of the stove and tugged on the odd clothes. They smelled like his mother's cedar closet. Somewhere the man resumed his rummaging.

"Boy." He called from the shadows. "Come here and get some boots and gloves. Where is she?"

"Down the road a bit, quarter mile, maybe. We saw the house. She wanted to come with me, but I thought this was better."

The old man grunted as he pulled on his boots, stamping his heels into them. Finished, he sat, collecting his breath. He wondered about his old truck in the barn. It probably wouldn't start, cold and unused as it had been since Tessa convinced the doctor to tell him not to drive. He was more confident about the Fordson tractor, was sure he could coax the gray old beast to life. But, aside from yanking the car from the ditch, it would provide no benefit over walking. This was no night to be crawling with tow chains under cars. Still, he remembered a time when he would have relished the idea.

They left through the side door, each swinging flashlights into the swirl. The old man broke trail until, embarrassed, the boy moved ahead of him. Even then, the old man steered him with a gloved grip on his shoulder, turning him down the driveway to avoid the ditch. Reaching the road, they stopped. The boy searched for his tracks, but the old man tapped his arm and pointed down the road where the car lights shone weakly, dimmed by the snow.

He had grabbed blankets and some of Tessa's old winter gear, but he should have remembered a shovel. They fell into the drift and kicked and scooped at the snow with their hands while the storm fought back, sucking their breath and erasing their progress. Twice he leaned against the car, gasping, the frozen air tearing his lungs. The boy worked resolute, until he finally jerked on the door and shouted for the girl to push. Together, the boy gripping the handle, the man tugging on the window frame, the girl shoving from inside, they inched the door open. They stuffed the blankets and clothing through the gap and waited, breathing hard in unison as she wrapped herself against the storm. With one final and unified heave they freed her.

His breath spent, his heart racing, he could not manage the ditch, and watched the kids scramble up together and stand on the road, waiting. He could barely shake his head. They jumped down, and one on each side, pinioned him forward in a mad frozen three-legged race to the road. They paused long enough for the boy to shout "Ready?" into his face, and when he nodded they continued. Making the house with their faces bent to the ground, the old man propped between them, guiding their steps by memory.

The house felt shockingly hot. They stripped off snow-plastered coats and staggered to the stove. After a time the girl made tea, fed the stove and engaged in soft and one-sided conversation. The boy brooded, his shame dulled only slightly by his part in the rescue. The old man listened and settled his breath. Closing his eyes, he could imagine her voice to be Tessa's or even his wife's, so many years ago.

He billeted the boy in his room and the girl in the one he kept for Tessa. He dismissed their protests, insisted he slept well and often in his chair. The boy suggested he and the girl could share a bed, but the old man, despite what they had been through, would not allow it.

In the morning he brewed coffee in an old percolator, and made them eggs and oatmeal on the gas stovetop. Together, the kids hauled in more wood for the fire. They sat and watched the storm die slowly. The old man thought again of the tractor. In his mind he walked through the steps required to start it in the cold, wondered about the tow chain, considered whether the boy could locate a secure grab point on the car. Finally, he reached for the phone and called the Stiefel farm. Early in the afternoon he watched Ben Stiefel help the boy, clad in borrowed Carharts, hook a strap from the buried car to the giant dual-wheeled John Deere. He smiled when the green

10

tractor, bold against the pale landscape, eased the buried car free. The boy pumped a gloved fist in victory.

The kids stayed until supper, until the swept sky, a hurtful blue all afternoon, faded indigo and the moon rose as if to survey the storm's handiwork. The county plow had pushed through an hour or two before, leaving a single lane perilous but clear. The boy itched to leave. The girl hugged the old man, flashed him a smile, and whispered thanks. The boy extended an awkward hand, soft and unscarred. He gripped it mightily, held it for a moment, then released it with a shake. He brushed aside their thank-you's and watched them drive away, marked their progress by the slow and tentative blinking of their brake lights.

He swung his chair to face the window and lit candles for company and light. The tea kettle sang and he scooped hot cocoa mix into a mug. Settling in his chair, he draped the blanket on his lap and watched stars dot the purpled sky. The chocolate steam rose from his mug and warmed his face. At the property line, the emerald spruces stood still and sentinel. The blanketed fields waited in stiff, brittle rows.

When Tessa called, he spoke only of the storm, as if he'd watched its passing from his chair. Spring, he assured her, was coming. A promise, certain and kind.

Honest, Faithful Graves

For a long time I looked for the living among the dead. For a long time I didn't realize that's what I was doing. At first, I thought I was honoring memories, showing respect for lives mostly forgotten. Later, I believed I was making a statement—visiting cemeteries, being comfortable there, I was testifying against fear. Death surrounds us, but we do our best to keep it distant, out of sight. We dance around the truth, or make a joke of it. Then we act surprised by its appearance.

So maybe I set out to remove death's mask, to remind us of what all those stones represent, to stop pretending that we can hide it behind rolling hills and iron gates and serene marble angels. The truth, though, is that I aimed too low.

Since I was a boy I have felt comfortable in cemeteries. Countenancing death was less heroic than circumstantial. I grew up a short block from a small township graveyard. My friends and I played around the stones with relaxed indifference, maintaining respectful distance only when mourners gathered around open graves. After each burial, we stayed away for a day or two, then slipped back in under the arched iron gate, whispering with adult-like solemnity. The sexton knew us, or our fathers at least, from his duties as janitor of our church. He seemed to enjoy our company, nodding and smiling at us as he mowed grass and moved sprinklers. Sometimes we watched him dig, carving out sharp-edged graves with a

13

rusting backhoe, or when the ground was too wet to support machinery, with shovel and pick. On those days we moderated our play among the silent stones and flowered urns, rarely straying from the graveled paths.

Back then, the suburbs were still miles away and the place felt set apart and ancient. I remember sprawling maples trunked so stoutly that it took three of us to stretch our arms around them. The oldest graves stood close to the road, arched chalky tablets marching up the hill. As the cemetery grew, so did the size and complexity of the markers, so that the hill's crest was studded by granite pyramids and shiny marble rectangles and one or two bronze angels. On hot summer days we packed baloney sandwiches and pickles and Boy Scout canteens filled with orange Kool-Aid, and, arriving at our destination, we'd cool our backs against the moss-speckled granite slabs. We played hide-and-seek and war under the banked green shade, or wandered from stone to stone, making family connections, calculating the shortest and longest life span, giggling over names like *Horatio* and *Marmaduke*. It was an odd playground. Our youthful laughter rung out over the silent monuments more honest, if less durable, than the tactile testimonies chiseled in stone. We weren't afraid. Nor do I think we intended irreverence. We were too young to suspect the enemy there. Rather, the more sensitive among us ran with a vague but increasing awareness of the sacred. Others recognized little more than time and grass and trees and stones.

It was usually three of us, my best friend Keith VanTil, the incredibly freckled Brian Bishop, and me. For a time a girl named Christi—I don't recall her last name—tagged along. She was a year or two younger than us and had a nose that never stopped running. She always carried an inhaler with her, puffing on it after playing too hard. Sometimes she just braced herself on a headstone and watched us play while she struggled for breath.

One summer a new kid named Kelvin moved down the street, a strange, bookish boy who actually read *National Geographic* for the science articles. We were into playing war that summer, acting out heroic scenes, hurling ourselves into the enemy lines like Pickett's doomed but glorious men. Except that we always prevailed. For a few days Kelvin watched our bloody game from the sidelines. When he asked to join we shrugged, explained the rules, and suggested that if he didn't own an appropriate plastic weapon a stick would do. Then he asked to be the enemy.

It was a new twist. Our enemies were always imaginary, an invisible force behind the hill. Giving them flesh and blood seemed like a fine idea. I'll admit to hesitating only because I wondered if this kid, with his crazy Einstein hair and mumbled speech, could really match up to our expectations. He was an unassuming adversary. Kelvin accepted our counsel with silent nods and then slunk off to take his position. For the next two days, he baffled us with a form of guerilla warfare we declared both inglorious and downright unfair. There were no lines to bravely charge. Instead, we found ourselves bewilderingly pinned down. Standing, we'd die. The only way to survive was to lay low and wait. Against a real enemy, our once glorious death was, well, inglorious, and mere survival was boring. We invented bullet-stopping force fields, but Kelvin just countered with equally fantastic weapons, only his were more believable. After two days we quit and switched to baseball. We didn't miss Kelvin much when his folks divorced and he moved away. We moved back to war.

I'm not sure when we stopped playing in the cemetery. I suppose it was a natural transition. Kelvin or no Kelvin, we played more sports. We noticed girls. We grew up, and our neighborhood cemetery began to gain all the normal connotations. Some of my school friends wanted to pull Halloween pranks there. Later, in high school, some kids went there late at night to party, but shied away during the day. It never made sense to me.

Now, I drive past a large municipal cemetery on my daily commute. It straddles both sides of the street, and a rare day passes without something to see. I roll along slowly, annoying other drivers, but I see more than they do. It is a busy place. Joggers and dog walkers use it as a safe route away from the busy street. Pairs of young mothers push strollers and chat. It serves as a park to them, just as a cemetery served as a playground for me and my boyhood friends. But just a few paces away, folks shake silently with grief.

People never get used to the dead among us. Driving past a cemetery, they keep eyes on the road, fiddle with the radio or suddenly remember an urgent and unreturned phone message. There are things to see even in the short glimpses offered at thirty five miles per hour: the long lines of flagged cars, the funeral tents, the head-bent mourners. But I'm more interested in what comes after the hearse leaves and the sexton rakes the soil flat. I watch for lonely cars idling in rain-drenched twilight, the grey-haired couple leaning against each other over a freshened grave, the bouquet of roses delivered after dark. Those are the stories I collect. Not the old ones. You won't find me making crayoned rubbings of engraved epitaphs, or sketching out the roots of sprawling family trees. It's the present I'm interested in, the stories that walk between the stones. The stories still unfolding. The mourners and the morbid. The curious and the convicted. They come here to hide as well as to remember. They come here to consider. I watch faces. I study postures. I wonder what brings them. I want to know what happens next.

Last autumn I saw a man and his dog sitting by a headstone. The man wore new denim bibbed overalls and a gray long-sleeved shirt. He hunched, seated on a small folding stool, his elbows propped on his knees. The wide flat brim of his straw hat shaded his face, but I imagined him to be old and outdoorsy—a farmer, maybe. Beside him a mostly black German shepherd stretched, snout on paws, staring ahead as intently as the man. I couldn't just drive by. I turned in, parked at a discreet distance, and watched.

It wasn't like when I was a kid. I was uncomfortable, slouching low behind the steering wheel, aware that I was intruding on a private moment. The man sat as still as the stones. From where I sat, I couldn't determine if he bowed his head in prayer, or if his gaze locked on a nearby headstone. The dog, ears flat and tail motionless, never flinched. Then, quite abruptly, the man stood, folded the stool, and spoke to his dog. They made their way to a gleaming red pickup truck and drove past on the way out. I wanted to express some sympathy, maybe wave respectfully, but instead I just nodded unnoticed behind my tinted windshield. I thought of trailing him, pulling up next to him at a traffic light and saying something—*I'm sorry for your loss*—but I stayed, watching the shadows unroll until an indigo squad car slipped past the entrance gate and turned my way.

For a few weeks I stopped each Thursday at the same time, hoping to see the dog and the man again. If I was brave enough, I thought, I would approach the man, maybe with a treat for the dog, and ask about his grief. After a few more weeks, my Thursday evening visits became my own ritual. Instead of waiting solely for the man and his dog, I formed a relationship with the *place*. Every mourner, no matter how solitary, deserves an observer. I stayed hidden. I kept a wall of glass between us. I didn't presume to share any burden. For a long time I was content just sitting there, waiting for no one and expecting nothing.

I stuck to the older sections of the cemetery, built before the practicalities of lawn maintenance dictated monument design. I like the aesthetic disorder of the old city plots, the towering obelisks and miniature Greek temples of dead industrialists, still competing with each other even while their bodies rot. Some bought themselves permanent mourners, marble maidens with pained expressions and faraway stares. A few strike poses that are less than chaste. Standing in the midst of them is a towering granite Jesus, his features worn after a century of weather and smog. His beard is chipped and one finger of his extended hand is missing.

There is nothing worse than the modern plots, where the markers are no more than plaques screwed to flat concrete slabs. From a car, it's easy to forget that graves surround you, that hundred of bodies turned to dust beneath you. Walking, you have to be careful not to stumble over some poor soul's sunken grave. I hate the place. It is too flat, too indifferent, artificial without the broken horizon cut by a hill of jagged headstones. What hills there are have been pushed in place by bulldozers rather than shaped for centuries by God. Squint a little and the place becomes a golf course. No mourners. No angels, stone or otherwise. A quiet grassy place to spread a picnic cloth or take a nap, a place to sleep comfortably among the dead.

An old drunk actually *did* sleep comfortably between two gravestones that hid his body. He played a clumsy game of cat and mouse with the local police, who prowled panther-like over the winding roads, guarding the dead. At first, they kept a close eye on me. A lone male in a parked car raises warnings. I started carrying a sketch pad and note book, telling them I was researching a book on headstones. Eventually I became part of the scenery, my gray Taurus as familiar as a monument.

Most nights I arrived after the workers left, but just in case I would wait near the gate until traffic slowed. Then I'd move deeper, frequently parking by the equipment shed. It sits past the crest of the largest hill, hidden by rows of towering spruces. I admired the utility of the place, the fading brown metal siding streaked with rust, the smell of diesel fuel and grease and fresh earth. Always the smell of earth, no matter the season. Two backhoes crouched behind the overhead doors. Compassionate practicality: the assurance that a grave would be dug regardless of mechanical failure. In the summer, when the nights stayed bright late, I pulled a folding chair from my trunk and sat with my back to the big garage doors. If there was a breeze the air filled with the minty smell of the trees. Sometimes it was so quiet I could hear the metallic tick of the lawnmower engines cooling in the shed.

It's there where I first saw her. It was one of those July nights when the air hangs stiff and the sun refuses to drag the day's heat down with it. I sat with my chair tucked into the scented shade of the spruce trees. Fireflies sparked among the stones. The last jogger had huffed through an hour ago. Somewhere, a chorus of sirens chased through the streets, edging closer and then fading toward the west. Birds nestled in the trees for the night.

I heard a car coming, a sputtering purr tracing the north entrance route, winding slowly back toward my hiding place. It rolled into view on my right, disappeared behind the big hill, and then reappeared on the other side. It paused at a fork in the road, idling. Then it lurched forward, crabbing down the gravel drive that curved in front of the equipment building. The car, a yellow, slouching import pocked with rust, slowed to a walk, stopped, then jerked with the spastic release of a worn out clutch. It died with a sputter, coughing a cloud of gray, oily smoke.

Rock music drifted from the open windows. For a long time, no one moved from the car. Then the driver's door creaked open and a tall, skinny kid stood, lit a cigarette, and stared up the hill. He wore a gray fedora stuffed over an explosion of red hair, tight jeans, and a dark gray t-shirt damp with sweat. He leaned back toward the window and said something to the passenger, shrugged and walked to the front of the car. He sat on the hood and smoked. When nothing remained but the filter, he flicked it aside, planted both hands on the hood and pushed off like a kid on a playground slide. He scuffed to the passenger side of the car, said something through the window, and jerked the door open.

The girl he coaxed out was thin and pale. She slipped past the boy without looking at him and stood, fidgeting her short black hair into a loose ponytail. She wore an oversized white t-shirt, knotted at the waist, and a pair of black satin gym shorts. The boy tugged a backpack from the car, pulled out a large camera rig and started up the hill. He talked rapidly as he walked, but I could not make out what he said. The girl followed slowly, picking her way around the headstones, pausing here and there as if interested in the inscriptions.

When she reached the boy, they stood facing each other and he continued his one-sided conversation, waving his hands and smiling widely, like a used car salesman in one of those shouting TV commercials. Finally, she shrugged and walked to a large limestone monument. It had a square stone about three feet wide. From the base, a tall fluted column rose like a fragment of an ancient Greek temple. The top of the column was missing. The girl climbed the base and stood facing the boy, her back against the stone. She shuffled a little, brushed her bangs aside, hugged her arms high across her chest.

The boy lifted his camera and began to shoot. He moved in a semicircle around the girl, kneeling, standing, climbing onto nearby stones to catch her from different angles. The girl stood, passive, dropping her arms, not really posing. When the boy talked to her she occasionally nodded, but remained silent. She only moved to brush hair from her face. After a while the boy began to shout. The girl responded slowly, stretching her arms out, hanging her head, bending at the knees. Whatever she tried, it didn't seem to please him. He moved close, grabbing her arms, twisting her at the waist. At that point it was impossible to understand what he was going for. Maybe an embarrassing imitation of a crucifix.

Next, the boy had her sit on the stone base, body limp, head bent awkwardly to one side. The girl's face looked white against the weathered gray granite. The boy took great care with these shots, changing lenses so he could zoom close. He posed the girl, lifting her limp arms and

21

repositioning them, tugging the fabric of her shirt a certain way, freeing her ponytail so hair draped her face. During all this, the girl never moved. It was almost dark. He gathered his things into the backpack and returned down the hill.

He packed his gear, muttering. He lit another cigarette, leaving it dangling between his lips as he scrolled the images on his camera display. Occasionally, he would glance up the hill where the girl sat, still as death, and shake his head or shout something in her direction. Then he climbed in the car, drove clumsily across the grass to the road, and disappeared around the hill.

I almost stood and ran after him. Instead, I sat watching the motionless girl fade to gray in the twilight, listening to the car accelerate away. She remained propped awkwardly on the stone. Fireflies danced brightly up and down the hill. I stood and folded my chair and leaned it against my car. I glanced at my watch. It was nearly ten. A firefly landed on my arm, folded its wings, and began to crawl, its glow fading. Unlit they are ordinary bugs. When I looked up, the girl was gone.

I got in my car and left. I drove slowly with the window down, looking and listening. There was no sign of her, just the lingering sulfured scent of boy-wonder photographer's ratty car. Winding my way back to the entrance, I began to hope I'd encounter a police car. I'd stop to shoot the breeze, casually mentioning what I saw. Then it would be out of my hands. Instead, I met no one on my way out, and little traffic all the way home. For the average soul it was a good night to stay inside.

I slept surprisingly well. I wish I could say that the girl troubled my sleep—that I woke frequently from haunting dreams. I didn't. I stayed up longer than usual, restless in

22

the stale air-conditioned room, but I don't remember much of the night. Instead, I woke with a feeling that I'd forgotten something important. The *what* hit me as soon as I got in my car. I drove distractedly, dialing my radio for the local news. Nothing. No bodies discovered in cemeteries. No missing persons. Passing the cemetery, I fought the urge to turn in. By now I was beginning to believe there was nothing to see.

But I did go back. I give myself credit for that. I resumed my regular schedule, stopping every other evening and spending at least a few minutes watching. The heat continued to keep people away. There was little to see. I stayed in the car with the windows up and the AC blowing. One night a bunch of teenage punks slouched past and heard my car running. They turned up the drive and strutted up to the car. The shortest, a spidery kid with hard eyes and a cheap grin, knuckled my window. Fingering the button, I inched the window open. "Hey, old man. How bout sharing some of that AC? Nice and cool in there." Two others stood staring behind him. A big shirtless kid sat on the fender. The car listed under his weight.

Shifting into gear, I told them I was just leaving. The short kid laughed and slapped the roof and the big one bounced the front of the car up and down before he slid off. Then they stepped aside and let me pass. I was shaking, glad to get away, but by the time I reached the entrance I realized I'd just given up my favorite spot. I returned on schedule in two days, but it wasn't the same. I'd compromised my place for the sake of air conditioning. After that I parked away from the building and walked. Rummaging through the junk behind the shed, I fashioned a chair out of an old tractor seat and a five gallon bucket. I made a shelter in the trees, breaking away branches so I could see. It was buggy and hot, but I grew to like the closeness of it.

The morning after I ran from the punks, I woke worried about the girl. I left early and drove to the back of the cemetery. At the shed, groundskeepers were already milling around idling mowers. I parked in the road and walked back to the monument where the girl had disappeared. No sign of the girl, or the wannabe photographer. Grey pitted stone, moss, bird droppings. Dandelions. Squirrel-chewed acorn husks.

The base was lettered on all four sides, each chiseled with names and dates. No verses, no promises of resurrection. No prophesies. Only the broken column pointing at the sky. Behind me, the mowers moved back and forth across the grass. I stood silently with my head down, the same posture I'd observed from a distance so many times before. I closed my eyes and conjured a picture of the girl crumpled on the monument.

As the mowers moved closer, I began walking in a loose circle, starting from the monument and spiraling through the individual graves. The problem was, I didn't know what to look for, or if I'd recognize a clue if I saw one. I was late for work for the first time in years.

One week later, the photographer returned. I was walking, the mosquitoes so thick I couldn't sit quietly in the trees, when I heard his car chug around the bend. I stood close to the trees and watched while he unloaded his gear and hauled it up the hill. This time he carried tripods and flash units and those light reflectors that unfold like umbrellas. He set up around the column-topped monument, tried a few shots, made some adjustments, and then sat on the stone block, dialing his cell phone. He smoked and paced and talked to himself. I began to hope he was waiting for the girl.

When the sun finally set, his pacing became frantic. He stalked to the top of the hill and stood looking toward the entrance. Then he marched back down, kicking headstones, trying at one point to pick up a heavy cement planter as if he wanted to hurl it at something. Failing, he seemed to settle some. He began to gather his gear, stacking it behind his car. I wandered down and stood at the edge of the road. He kept packing, muttering under his breath.

"I saw you up there. You think you're hidden, but I saw you," he said. He talked without looking up from his work. "Sitting up there, taking it all in. Woulda gave you a show tonight, man." He looked toward me and grinned. "A fine show."

"I was wondering about the girl."

"Yeah, aren't we all. Told her to be here an hour ago. Paid her in advance. Damn expensive, too."

"Then she's all right?"

"All right? She's premium material. The real deal. Usually works in Chicago, even LA, but a friend swore she'd do me a favor. Would've lit this place up." He leaned against the trunk and lit another cigarette, tipped his head back and exhaled through his nose. "*All right*?" He snorted. Smoke snaked from his nostrils.

"She didn't look so well. Then you just left her." I said. He looked at me puzzled, then he laughed.

"You mean that skinny whore a week ago? Hell knows where she is. Picked her up at a bar after she told me some lies about modeling experience. I liked her look. Pale. Sweet but ragged. Then she just stands there. Had to spell

25

everything out for her. *Every damn thing.*" He dropped the smoking butt, ground it under his heel, and lit another. "Had an idea when I saw her. Turned out to be a bad one. This one, though, she's the real deal."

I stood and watched him smoke. He glanced at his watch, rechecked his phone, finished his smoke and flicked it aside. It fell smoldering in the grass. "Well, another time, I guess. Some other chick, too." He laughed. "Shame, though. Would've been something to see. Would've shook this place up. Ha. Practically raised the dead, old man." As if to prove his point, he picked up his camera and pushed the shutter. Light exploded from two tripod-mounted flash units still aimed at the monument. Then he turned away and resumed packing.

I shrugged and walked away in a curving, indirect route that took me up the hill. At the crest, I watched a taxi bounce over the speed bump just past the entrance gate and turn in our direction. It drove around the hill and stopped behind the photographer's rusted heap. He stopped packing and nearly ran to meet it. He looked in the backseat, let out a *whoop* and quickly paid the driver.

The kid was right; the woman was beautiful. She emerged from the taxi like a star stepping onto red carpet, smoothing the creases from her skirt as she stood. Even without her spike-heeled boots she would've towered over the kid. He looked up at her and, as dark as it was, I could see his satisfied, toothy smirk. He shook her hand and fawned, a minor priest before her presence.

He guided her to the monument and she mounted it without instruction. From where I stood, I couldn't see much of her, but whatever she was doing set cameras flashing. The kid fired off shot after shot. I began inching down the hill, angling in the shadows until I stood a little behind the kid's car.

The model began shedding clothes, wrapping bare arms and legs around the column, leaning away from it, her twisting poses drawing moans of delight from the frantic photographer. With each explosion of light, the headstones behind her flashed, their polished faces gleaming like black mirrors. *He was right*, I thought, but it made me sad to think it.

I felt pinned down that night, as if my old neighbor Kelvin stalked the shadows, calmly calling out death from behind every headstone, and there wasn't anything I could do about it. I thought about the old man and the dog, and a hundred other mourners I had studied as they bore their silent pain and hopes in flower baskets and helium balloons. I thought of the gang of kids with their violent postures and insincere grins. I tasted something foul and black at the back of my throat. Overhead, the trees buzzed with the chainsaw cries of a million cicadas. I grabbed the fender of the car and bent over, ready to be sick.

Instead, I began to walk. Eyes on the ground, I stumbled in the direction of the monument. I started picking up the model's clothes, while the camera continued to flash. Somewhere, I suppose, there are images of me handing clothes to a partially clad woman cowering behind a headstone. Suddenly shy, she hid behind the column, yelling at the photographer to get "That creep away from me!"

After that it becomes blood and sirens and flashing red lights and cops scratching on note pads. Before that, though, I was hit or shoved hard against the monument. For whatever reason, the pillar fell. Maybe the model was leaning away as I crashed into it, maybe it was just time for it to fall. I blacked out for a few minutes. When I came to, the pillar lay broken. Some of its pieces had rolled down the hill. Toppled light stands and tripods lay scattered and bent.

I sat on the broken remains of the column, sweating. Next to me, the model shivered, wrapped in a police blanket. Under the red police lights, she looked older than I had imagined. The cops had the kid handcuffed, but he kept grinning and asking for a cigarette. An officer told us we would need to meet with some detectives in the morning. I offered the woman a ride, but she emerged from her stupor, sneered, and shook her head. "Like I want to see your face a minute longer." She said a few other choice things. Revived, she strutted off on bare feet, carrying her boots. I don't know how she got home, or wherever she was headed.

The cop stood for a long time just staring at me, then shook his head and sat. "You," he sighed, "Are a strange one. Never could figure out why you hang around this place. I never believed your story about writing a book."

"I appreciate your tolerance." I meant it sincerely, and if it came out sarcastic the officer didn't seem to notice.

"I think it would be wise to stay away."

"I will. Let things settle for a while."

"No. Not a while. I don't think you'll be welcome here, not until you arrive in a box, like the rest of these folks." His radio crackled and he listened, fingered a button, and spoke a few cryptic words in response. Then he stood and looked down at me. "Most of us, you know, try to avoid this place."

I took his advice. Mostly. Twice a week I parked at a church down the block and walked the side streets to the back of the cemetery. A rusted iron fence hidden under a row of weeping willows still guards that part of the cemetery. I found an opening parted by a heavy tangle of wild vines and for weeks I returned and watched from under those trees, until the leaves turned yellow and then brown. I visited less during the winter, but I still came at least once a week, pushing through knee-deep snow, walking the fence line.

There was nothing to see. No one visited. The fresh graves were dug in the newer sections, behind the hills. Finally, I wiggled out a few fence stakes to make an opening. Climbing through, I trudged across the unmarked snow and worked my way back to the equipment shed. The tractor seat was still propped among the trees. I dragged it out and carried it to the front of the shed, where I had a clear view of the hill. I shaded my eyes and searched for the place the girl had danced and disappeared. Without its column and draped with snow, the monument was hard to distinguish from all the others on the hill. The road there was plowed irregularly, traced with the rutted tracks of the service vehicles, but beyond its edges the snow stretched stark and unbroken. I walked down the drive and across the road, but I stopped at the banked edge. The last snow had fallen days ago, and wind and sun had hardened it into rounded waves of dull white marble. I wanted to walk on it, to feel my weight supported for an instant and then, with a dull crunch, break the surface and sink. Something stubborn blocked me, held my feet to the ground, and I knew I couldn't go any farther. It was a place asleep. I didn't belong.

In late February a warm spell tugged people out of their winter stupor and I joined them, wandering the cemetery freely. Melting snow slid from headstones and folks walked hatless, jackets unzipped against the cold, testifying to the promise of spring despite a definite nip in the air. I was near the entrance when I saw a bright red pickup turn through the gate and park. The old man and his dog climbed down and walked stiff-legged to the grave. He unfolded his stool and coaxed the dog to lie down. I leaned against a tree and watched, glad the old man was back, glad his dog was at his side. I was ready to leave, determined that this time I would walk away before they did, so that I could remember them sitting there, grieving. I felt so sure and righteous that when I saw a runner approach I bristled, ready to confront her, to turn her away so they could mourn in peace. I would have, too. But seeing the man, she stopped, and breathing deep and easy, stood with her hands propped on her hips. She was thin, strong, cheeks flaring pink against her pale skin. She walked quietly and knelt between them. With one hand she scratched the dog's perked ears. The other she laid gently on the old man's shoulders. At her touch, he looked up, tipped his big straw hat, and nodded a greeting. Then surprised, he stood and placed his hands on her shoulders and pulled her close. For just a moment, I thought I recognized her, too.

They walked, the old man gimpy and bent, the woman matching his pace, her hand gently brushing the big dog's ruff. Twice she jogged ahead. The dog raced after her, circled, then loped back to the old man. The second time the dog stayed at his side and she waited until they caught up.

I followed at a distance, but when the woman spotted me I stopped. She studied me. The man and the dog reached her and she let them pass. The red pickup was parked near a big pile of pushed snow. I watched her breath leave her mouth in great clouds and hang in the air like a testimony. Then she smiled and turned and jogged after the others.

I turned too, and walked slowly back to where I'd first spotted them. Row after row of headstones stood in the melting snow glistening, and my mind tuned to spring. I noticed their colors, pearl gray, and sapphire blue, black as deep as onyx, the soft pink of a tulip bud. The old man had forgotten his stool. I sat, placed my feet in the hollows left by his boots, propped my elbows on my knees. The stone in front of me was swept clear of snow. I read the name, the date of birth, the date of death. I numbered the years. Far away, truck doors slammed, an engine started, tires slipped and then caught on the damp pavement. Lifting my head, I saw dozens of names chiseled in stone or cast in bronze, lives marked by dates and family tree, summed up in a line or two of type. I was suddenly alone. The walkers were gone home. I wanted to see kids darting from tree to tree, I wanted to see Kelvin popping up, demanding that I play fair and die. I wanted to see weak Christi, pale and propped on a grave marker, watching us play. I wanted. Instead, I saw footprints in the snow, steam rising from the sun-warmed face of the gravestone. I leaned close and I began to weep, waiting, in spite of myself, for a stranger's embrace.

Sand, Smoke, Current

The boy had thought about the dam all day. During class he doodled in the margins of his textbooks and glanced often outside at the cloud-scudded sky, worrying about rain. At recess, he skipped baseball to search the library for books on dam building. Even with the librarian's help, he left with only one thin picture book of the Hoover dam. It was hard to imagine any practical use for it, but he pondered it through science and geography and the final chapter of *The Bridge to Terabithia.* He was still daydreaming as the bus's tires crunched the graveled shoulder and the driver cranked the big chrome handle, folding the door open.

He gathered his lunch box and, nodding at the driver, swung down the steps. Halfway up the sloping drive he saw the truck and remembered it was Thursday, his father's afternoon off. He would have to ask permission to borrow the shovel. The driveway ended at the top of a hill where it curved to meet the white clapboard garage. Behind the garage, his father stood in the middle of a freshly-tilled garden, his back to the boy. A greasy brown rototiller crouched nearby. Next to it, a transistor radio crackled out a Tigers baseball game. The air smelled of topsoil and gasoline and the hot-oiled workings of the rototiller.

His father pitch-forked the soil, lifting clumps of dirt and sifting until the tines held only a tangle of roots. These he flung aside and then plunged the fork back into the

33

earth. He paused, dragged a dirty handkerchief from the pocket of his brown work pants, and wiped his bald, sun-pinked head. The lazy drone of the radio faded to static. Turning toward it, he spotted the boy standing at the edge of the garden.

"Hi, son. You startled me." He smiled and crossed the tilled rows to the grass. "How was school?"

"Okay, I guess."

His father glanced at the radio, then back at the boy.

"We should play catch after supper," the father said. "I need to finish the garden, or we could do it right now. Deal?"

"Sure." The boy shrugged. "Do you want help?"

His father unrolled a squashed cigarette pack from his left sleeve and shook his head.   "Naw, you go on. That old quackgrass and me, we got our own personal argument. Every spring I root it out. Every summer it creeps back in. Adam's curse, I guess."

"Okay." The boy squared his skinny shoulders. "Can I borrow the shovel?"

"I guess so. Not building tunnels are you? Remember that boy who got buried doing that? Your mom'll ground us both if she finds out I let you use the shovel for that kind of nonsense."

"No. I'm building a dam. Back of the pit. I'm trying to make a beaver pond."

"If there were beavers around here, they'd build their own." His father kneeled by the radio, fussing with the dial. Satisfied, he looked back at his son. "Dam, huh? Built a few myself. Never lasted, though. Current always wins. Go ahead, take the shovel." He pointed a soiled finger at

34

the boy. "Don't lose it. Not like my ratchet wrench." He tapped the boy's freckled cheeks with a sandy fist and walked back into the garden.

The boy retrieved the shovel from the garage and laid it on his shoulder. He marched past the garden and followed a narrow path that angled down the back of the hill, through a greening field of Timothy grass and Queen Anne's lace. The trail ended at a steep bank, then dropped several feet to a wasteland of blow sand. Jumping down, the boy advanced across the sand, occasionally shifting the shovel from one shoulder to the other.

He retraced his old zigzagging tracks up a steep sand pile and skidded down the other side. Below, the stream spread several feet wide. It ran shallow—barely ankle deep. He kicked off his shoes and eased into the water.

The dam had failed, of course. The current had carved a wide slash through it, but behind it the water spread deeper, eddying slow and foamy before it finally spilled through the opening. The boy smiled. Then he jabbed the shovel's blade into the sandy bank and set about repairing the breech.

Steep sand piles formed a wall around him and he heard only the water's soft chuckle, the suck of the sand sliding off the shovel's blade, his own jagged breath. He did not hear his father's call and only vaguely registered the persistent honking of a distant car horn. It was the smell of tobacco that caused him to lean on the shovel and look around.

His father squatted on the bank, masked in the long evening shadows, a skinny cigar clamped in his teeth. Smoke clouded his face and curled downstream. "Dam looks good." He pulled the cigar from his mouth and held

35

it suspended between his knees. *Special occasions, only,* his father always said. His mother hated them, so he saved them for small and private victories.

"I need to keep working."

"No, Mom wants you home. Besides, it'll get cold soon. Time to pack it in. After supper we can still get in a few tosses."

"Dad, it almost held last night. I can make it last if I work a little longer. I'm curving it like the Hoover dam. I'm making it strong."

His father studied the dam, looked at the boy, and glanced westward over the hill. He shook his head. "It's a fine feat of engineering, especially for a ten-year old, but it can't hold. The water will keep rising. Then what?" He stood, puffed hard one more time on the plastic tip of the cigar. He gave it a look and dropped it at his feet. "Nope, it's fine to try, but it's also good to know when something's bigger than you." He laughed. "Like me. Now come on. Let's get some supper."

They walked downstream. The father carried the shovel and the boy his shoes and neither said much. At supper, the boy remained silent, listening half-interested while his father praised the meal and spoke proudly of the dam and then of his garden. After supper they tossed a baseball until the light was spent and his mother declared bedtime.

Upstairs in his room, he listened to the soft murmurs of conversation drifting through the floor vent, the turning of locks, water running in the bathroom. When all was silent except the creaking of the old house, he slipped down the stairs. In the garage, he fished a chrome flashlight from his father's toolbox and lifted the shovel from its hook. Stars lit the trail and turned the sandpit into a shadowed moonscape. The only sound was the scuff of his rubber soles against the sand.

He knelt at the creek where his father had smoked and trained the flashlight along the dam and over the silvered pond. The water appeared motionless, but the boy knew not to trust it. He snapped the light off and waited, the shovel propped against one knee. Nestled there in the dark and cold, he fought sleep, nodding and twitching until the flashlight slipped from his hand. Reaching for it, he spotted the ivory stub of his father's cigar. He picked it up, wiped it clean on his pant leg, and, clamping it in his teeth, tasted the strange sweetness of his father's breath. He heard a trickle, then the steady, furious rush of water, and considered what his father had said about the beavers and the dam, how the current always wins. For a moment he hesitated, then he stood, hefted the shovel, and marched into the stream.

Knee deep in the black, splashing water, he scooped wet sand from the stream bed, slopping slick shovelfuls into the gap. The breech narrowed. The water roiled, angry. Changing tactics, he scrambled to the bank, levering the shovel deep into dry sand. Too heavy to carry, he dragged it across the top of the dam, back and forth, until the water slowed to a trickle, until the sound of his breath was louder than the current. He didn't rest. Or see the figure squat at the top of the hill, light flare behind cupped hands. Or smell the gray smoke that lifted, caught in the cool breeze, and drifted unseen above the boy's head and over the dam.

How to Stop a Freight Train

What was is no more. What was is no more. That thought clung to him like a sandbur to a sock. He tried reciting it, first as a whisper, then in rising tones of mock importance, laughing at his own cleverness. Even spitting the words in disgust, he failed to purge them. They formed the cadence he walked to, echoing in every gravel crunching step. He adjusted stride, his soft-soled shoes planted squarely on the railroad ties, but only the timbre changed. The chant marched with him, a grim and persistent companion.

Twenty minutes ago he'd parked his rental car and waited while the air-conditioned interior grew tepid in the sun. Ranks of *For Sale or Lease* signs competed for attention up and down the street. The same scenery he saw across the entire Midwest, suburban industrial parks ubiquitous as dandelions, just not as resilient. Emptied temples of steel and glass, hollow monuments to hard work. Liquidated dreams. Rotted by forces as unaccountable as shadows, propped up by failing optimism, and finally—at his arrival—bulldozed into bankruptcy. They always called him too late, too late to lecture on the virtue of caution and the calculating fear of the unknown. He sat numb on every flight, then donned sympathy like a necktie for every meeting with battered owners and worried employees, shed it again outside their door. He was not, he told himself, the executioner. He was the dismantler, the clean-up man, the euthanizer of dying

39

dreams. Still, parked in his old neighborhood, on the street where he grew up, he sensed the need to feel. He stepped from the car and stood for a long time. Then he started walking, retracing a thousand boy-sized steps, a suit-and-tied shadow wandering the tracks and muttering.

Almost three decades ago he ran through fields now buried under faded, cracked asphalt. Thirty years since he and his buddies played among the rising steel beams sprouting like promises from the dormant farmland. He remembered running up piles of earth, standing with raised arms, a dust-covered, temporary king of the hill. They wandered along the railroad tracks, collecting loose spikes, placing dull brown pennies on the polished rails. Then they would wait, filling time with talk of wars and baseball and girls, hoping the crushing weight of the locomotives would squeeze the coins paper-thin and bright. After the freight train passed they would scour the tracks for their treasure. The best and rarest finds lay curled like shiny metallic tongues. More often the coins would shimmy off the rail intact. Some simply vanished. The boys would laugh at their discoveries, then bury them in their jean pockets. By supper time, they were forgotten prizes. On laundry day his mother would collect them in an empty margarine dish she kept on top of the clothes dryer. Standing here, now, he wondered what happened to all that twisted currency.

The telegraph poles he remembered, wires drooping like slack harp strings, were gone, but the tracks followed the same gently curving path, draped like a beauty contestant's sash across the landscape. He passed drying wetlands, tall stands of rusting cattails, two precocious and shrill redwing blackbirds hopping stalk to stalk. To his right shuttered warehouses hunkered-down among encroaching weeds. He remembered, age nine, watching a stubborn farmer plant corn while bulldozers peeled back his neighbors' fields. It seemed an admirable act of defiance at the time.

He felt his phone buzz, fished it from his coat pocket and read the brief message. *Meeting running long. Sorry! Still have time? Maybe an hour?* He imagined her sitting upright, her phone tucked discreetly under a conference table, manicured nails clicking out the message. Her tailored skirt would pull tight across her lap, the hem stopping halfway up her tan thighs; her sleeveless blouse, tasteful and feminine, framing the soft curves of her shoulders and neck. She would wear her hair up. He preferred it hanging dark and loose across her shoulders. Wondered what it would feel like dangling in his face.

He stopped walking and concentrated. The words wouldn't line up. He deleted phrase after phrase, too long, too clever, too direct. A familiar thrill knotted tight and settled in his gut. *Better to wait,* he thought, and started walking again. He'd given up trying to figure out if she really wanted him, a man with receding hair and widening waist. And a wife. But after weeks of playful hints and veiled flirtation, he was determined to see where it led. Stopping, he sat across the track, one rail his seat, the dust-shaded toes of his dress shoes angled against the other. Sweat trickled under his shirt and collected in the folds of his waist. Shrugging out of his jacket, he laid it over his lap and rolled up his sleeves. He started tapping a new message. The little bare spot at the back of his scalp itched and baked.

The first vibrations registered in his toes, a soft warning humming through the rails. He turned from his phone and stared to the west. An indigo shadow floated blurred and liquid over the heat-shimmered tracks. He watched it grow—metallic shoulders squared and hard—until the ground pulsed under his feet and he stood and turned to face it. The train sounded its warning at a distant crossing and rushed on. He calculated, guessing speed and distance. He remembered standing on the tracks as a boy and listening to the others brag about how close they would let the train come before they jumped off the track. No one ever did what they predicted. He could see himself, young, silent, gauging the other boys, knowing they wouldn't live up to their bravado. Always wishing someone would.

Hooking his jacket with his thumb, he swung it over his shoulders. The train reached the bottom of the long grade, its twin locomotives chased by a line of freight cars tapering to the west. He smiled at the sound, the clear sonic pulsing of the generators, the diesel engines growling low and resonant. A mile away crossing bells began to clang and the gates swung down.

The train clambered closer, larger, until he could read the railroad logo in the dirty white circle on the nose, the number boards set like eyebrows above the cab windows. He imagined the engineer cursing under his breath, warning the other crew members of the idiot on the track. His phone buzzed, but he ignored it. It stopped, vibrated again, this time the slower rhythm of a voice mail message. He crossed his arms, uncrossed them, wedged them in his pockets, finally let them hang loose at his side. To his left the roadbed fell away steeply into a dirty drainage ditch. The right side was no more inviting, a harsh incline lined with heavy brush. He grinned and shook his head, deciding that his nine-year-old self would have picked a better place to make a stand.

The train hammered forward. *Focus on details; hand rails, air hoses, rust-stained bolt heads, shadowed faces, black heat and roar.* He leaned forward, shifted his weight like a sprinter ready to bolt. He picked a spot, his line in the gravel, waited for the train's black shadow. Every molecule in his world throbbed to the same hammering beat.

He proved no braver than his boyhood buddies. The train blasted one drawn-out warning long before it reached his imaginary line, slapped his bravery aside and launched him in an ugly stumble headlong down the sloping gravel. Scrambling to salvage some dignity, he climbed to his knees and faced the passing train. He expected some reaction, the engineer furiously mouthing curses behind the soiled glass, an enraged blast of the airhorn, the hiss of engaged brakes, but the train rolled past, blank and indifferent. Rising, he scrambled over the loose stones until he stood eye level with the track. The train clattered by, a steady stampede of steel, giant springs squeaking, tensioned-iron moaning at each dip in the roadbed, all weight, all unstoppable power. The rails rose and fell; ties lifted slightly from their gravel beds. Here and there a spike inched upward. He calculated the thousands required to anchor everything in place, stood still until the last car passed and the sound faded to a distant clicking metronome. Then he followed.

There was no sign of his jacket. His battered hands stung. One pant leg flapped open at the knee. He jerked his tie from his neck, unbuttoned his shirt, tugged it from his waist. It billowed out like a damp sail. Remembering his phone, he pulled it from his pocket and scrolled through the call log. There were two calls from clients, one from the airline. A voice mail from his wife. He cleared her message without listening. Opening the texting screen, he deleted his draft and started again. He tapped a few words —nothing clever, and he did not care—hesitated, then clicked send. Finished, he powered off his phone and set it carefully on the still-hot rail.

A pile of discarded railroad ties lay in the field. He crunched down the graveled bank and sat watching the track, waiting. A spike protruded from a tie near his foot and he wiggled it free from the rotting wood. The rusted iron felt warm and heavy and rough. He suspended it loose between thumb and forefinger, tapping it lightly with his wedding ring. It sounded a faint and distant warning.

Love, Double-barreled

Jacqueline Turner had an eye patch and a shotgun and a front porch. She wore the patch over her left eye and draped her shotgun over her lap, as comfortable as a quilt. She had a rocking chair, too. It waited, its cane seat vacant, reserved for a guest. Jacqueline preferred to survey the world from a chair with steady feet and a straight back, one without arms to hinder the swing of the gun. Her chair sat close to the door and tight to the wall, tucked neat within the morning shadows that cloaked her like a stage curtain. Seated there, she held court from first light until the sun swung high and pushed the shadows to her feet. Then she would rise, her posture bent to the form of the chair and shuffle into the house for a quiet lunch.

From the porch she monitored the general decline of her world, nature's slow and steady reclamation. With no respect for property lines or fences, and little sympathy for her waning physical strength, the land pushed inward on all sides. Maple saplings sprouted in her perennial beds. Poison ivy crept insidiously through her vegetable garden. Dandelions and thistles rampaged her lawn. Each fall the surrounding trees cast down blankets of leaves which winter flattened into a slick rubbery mat, a barrier to spring growth. Elsewhere, green woody life sprouted unordered, rising even from the valleys and gutters of the old house's roof. Sumac and sassafras sprung up around the foundation of her garden shed, locking arms against her entrance. Her weapons—shovels and hoes and axe— hung beyond her reach, patient with rust. Watching it with one eye, Jacqueline believed the randomness of nature followed a malicious, even diabolic plan.

Once she had been a lover of all seasons. Winter was her time of waiting, like a bride in the months before her wedding. During the day, she tramped through the snow-hushed woods with expectant steps. At night she planned, searching garden books and magazines, ordering seeds, making long lists lettered in flowing script. Restless, she filled pots with soil and planted. When spring burst, trilliumed and dogwooded, her window sills already danced with pale green shoots waiting for transplant. She would rush outside in high rubber boots, raking and shoveling the soil, letting it breathe the freshened air. Kneeling, she would crumble the loamy dirt through her fingers, the smell rolling inside her like incense. She had danced, frantic and lustful, with spring, until summer stepped in and pulled her into its muggy embrace. July came and swung her work deliberate and slow, hot hours of staking and weeding and coaxing, sweat-stung eyes, sun-burnt shoulders, knees stained soil-black. Come night, though, she would sit in the midst of the steamy growth, walled in by a chorus of crickets and tree frogs, the moon-silvered plants her silent companions. She sat so still that she could hear them breathe. It was a sweet lingering that lasted midway through August. Then she plunged back into earnest pace until fall. In autumn she rebelled, fighting killing frost with tarps and piling leaves into smoking mountains that she would burn in defiance, for one brief moment turning the dull and moldy brown back to blazing yellow and orange. She left her gardens neat and ordered, ready for winter's sleep.

That was another era—almost another woman. Now she watched every season with suspicion. Betrayed, she knew winter was just a long aching cold, something to be endured. Spring an unordered joke, untended flowers blooming hidden, poking through last year's decay and choked by weeds. Summer an onslaught, the ever-creeping strangulation that overwhelmed all her years of work. Fall a cascade of dying.

Her shotgun was a comfort. A dark and heavy thing, cold-blued steel bedded in walnut. It reminded her of shovels and hoes, the smooth wood silken against her palms, the barrels hard like a shovel head. Jacqueline loved to heft it from its hooks on the wall and carry it through the door. She would ease into her seat and lay it across her lap. As if, had she wanted to, she could raise it in threat and stop the world. To ensure its efficacy, and to expand her sense of control, she kept it oiled and waxed so the action snapped open and closed smartly. Trigger and safety clicked with precision. Each evening she broke the breech, removed the chambered shells, and ran an oiled wad through the barrels. Each morning she inserted the same brass-shouldered rounds and snapped the barrels closed.

She couldn't remember the last time she fired the gun, but she still remembered why she bought it. For two summers she had dueled with a persistent groundhog. It showed her no respect, staring languidly at her shouts, deftly dodging thrown stones, and relentlessly destroying her plants. It lumbered, ugly and indifferent, unlike the rabbits and ground squirrels and birds, pests she saw as noble and controllable. Those she fenced and trapped and startled. The groundhog was a beast unstoppable.

So, the next time she went to town, she stopped in the hardware store and asked for advice. Sam listened and smiled and stared shyly over her shoulder while she vented. He discussed traps and poisons and offered firearms as a final resort. She was ready for the final resort and seized upon it with unholy delight. She test-shouldered an assortment of rifles and shotguns, sighting murderously down their barrels. Finally she settled on a double-barrel, twenty-gauge Savage. It felt right in her hands; the name fit her mood. It had two triggers, one for each barrel, and fell open for loading with the simple slide of a lever.

She bought a box of shells and, upon Sam's insistence, a deluxe cleaning kit, that he promptly demonstrated. Imagining encouragement in her earnest eyes, Sam offered to take her to dinner and afterward shooting practice, just so she'd know how. But she declined gracelessly, leaving Sam nothing but the lingering earthy scent of her. *Poor, desperate old widower*, she thought.

She tried the gun first on a milk carton, pressing the stock firm against her shoulder, repeating Sam's instructions in a whispered chant. *Point, use the little round bead between the barrels as a guide,* trying to understand what Sam meant when he said you aim a rifle, but you point a shotgun. She finally sucked in a breath, held it, squeezed the trigger. Nothing happened. Embarrassed, she thumbed the safety forward and tried again. A loud blast. The gun slammed her shoulder and jerked upward. The milk carton stood untouched. She shifted her finger to the rear trigger, adjusted her stance, and fired again. When she opened her eyes, paper fragments drifted where the carton had stood. After that, she carried the gun with her while she gardened.

The groundhog evaded her the entire summer, digging madly when she wasn't looking, laying in wait when she watched. She was convinced that he smelled her bloodlust. Her hatred hibernated through winter, blanketed by the banked snow and dull sky. When spring came, she had almost forgotten him, the gun just another wall decoration. But when she found the first burrow beside the garden shed, the fresh dirt fanning out in a neat flat mound, her rage returned. Balling her fists, she retreated to the house to rearm.

She began to sit for hours in the shadowed porch, waiting. She was an impatient hunter. Twice, distracted by her flowers, she missed him. Thereafter she trained her mind to blank out the colors, turning everything to black and white. She learned to watch for the misstep, the plant twisting upwind, the dark stain of disturbed soil.

The next time she sighted him, he was standing aside his hole sniffing the air. The gun seemed to rise on its own, bending her forward so its barrels barely cleared the railing. It bucked in her hands before she was ready, a clumsy shot that nearly knocked her from her seat. The pellets whacked harmlessly against the shed. The ground hog stretched higher, turned his bullet-shaped head from side to side and ducked just as she squeezed the second trigger. This time she saw dirt fly. The beast jerked and turned and disappeared down the hole.

She flew off the porch, breaking the gun open as she ran, spent shells and smoke trailing behind her. At the hole, she fished shells from her pocket and reloaded. Dirt spattered the shed wall, a few pellet holes poked the cream siding. She saw blood, a dark smudge in the soil, spatters on the wall. Hardly a mortal wound, she thought, but it excited her. She slammed the breech shut, stepped back, angled the shotgun at the hole, and fired twice. Ears ringing, she crouched, peering into the dust-clouded burrow. Then she pulled a shovel from the shed and packed dirt in the hole for good measure.

In the morning she resumed her watch. Her hands still smelled of gunpowder; the air of victory. She found it hard to sit. By the afternoon she stood deep in her garden, hurling herself at her neglected plants like a guilty mother back from a long vacation. The shotgun straddled the handles of her wheelbarrow. When day ended, she cradled it inside, cleaned it, and hung it reverently in place. The next day she left it hanging on its pegs.

Wheeling a barrow-load of mulch that afternoon, she saw something crawling across the yard. Dropping the wheelbarrow handles, she advanced, shovel brandished like a spear. The beast maintained slow and crabbing progress, rear legs lifeless, front legs clawing the turf, small black eyes determined. Jacqueline paused, watching the creature edge its way across her yard. Then, as a tiny seed of pity began to grow, she raised the shovel high and beat the animal, pounding until its round mouth flattened in a blood-tinged grin. Gripping it by the tail, she dragged it deep into the woods. She held the memory precious through that summer. Recalling it when she gripped a shovel a certain way. Still, sometimes she woke in the dark, wondering if the ground hog had kin. If its burrows remained empty.

Nine months later her niece, an overzealous nursing student, convinced her to see a doctor about a few suspect sores on her face. Biopsies and treatments followed. She shouldered them gamely—figured it a fair reckoning for years in the sun—and, when she remembered, began to don long-sleeved blouses and wide-brimmed hats.

A routine eye exam revealed a malignancy in her left eye. It was winter. She submitted to the scalpel almost eagerly, determined to be healthy before spring. The surgeon found more than expected. When Jacqueline came to, her niece, who family had appointed to break the news, told her she had lost her eye and significant tissue around it.

Jacqueline gained a vicious hatred of the sun. Spring approached layered with chemo and radiation and dread. She returned to the garden sunscreened, hatted, long-sleeved, wrap-around sunglasses shielding her remaining eye. She saw the world awkwardly through only one eye. She stumbled, bumping into fence posts and trees. Her garden tools doubled as canes. Even the familiar porch steps demanded caution. Once she fell and lay in the grass for a long time, smelling its sweetness, stroking it. "I will not go through all that just to break my hip," she said out loud. Jaw set, she dragged herself up and hobbled inside. The garden shrank in size and priority, choked with weeds, withered in the heat. She resumed her old pose on the porch, gun across her lap, scanning her yard for shadows. She waited for the old rotting beast's offspring, ready to visit the sins of the father on the children. Waited so long she almost forgot what she was watching for.

She was watching when the young man appeared on her driveway, clipboard in hand, his eyes on the gravel drive. He looked up as he mounted the steps, stopped, placed his foot gingerly on the porch. The old woman sat shadowed under a stiff straw hat, slippered feet flat to the floor, shotgun tucked tight to her waist. He propped his clipboard on his knee and rattled a few pages. He cleared his throat. The old woman's chin dipped.

"Good morning," he said.

She stared. The boy smiled, trying hard to ignore the shotgun and the eye patch. "I'm here for the county health department." He flicked the ID badge that hung from a cord around his neck. "To make you aware of the dangers of lead paint. Your house probably has lead paint. May I talk to you about it?" The old woman nodded and waved him up, pointing at a rocker occupied by a large cat. The boy stepped toward the chair, stopping to calculate the trajectory of the shotgun. Then he took a breath and inched toward the chair, where he paused again, pondering the cat. It stared at him and then stood, arched its back, yawned and dismounted as silent as smoke. The boy sat, glanced at his clipboard and turned to the woman.

"Ms. Turner?" He asked.

"I am," She said.

"I'm Nick. I don't usually work for the county. I'm a summer intern." He watched her stare out at her yard. "Do you know about the dangers of lead paint? I don't need to take a lot of your time. I can look around and make some suggestions, or I can just leave you some brochures."

"I know about lead." She said and swiveled her head to look at him. Nick nodded. He felt his gaze shifting from the patch to the twin black orbs of the shotgun and back to her good eye. "I don't have any children to crawl around and eat paint chips, you know."

"No, probably not. And if you did, it sounds like you know something about lead paint. Of course there's more to know than just not to eat the chips. There's dust from old window sashes. Remodeling needs to be handled in special ways. Do you plan to remodel someday, Ms. Turner?" She was searching the yard again, her head swiveling, slow and deliberate. Nick studied the peeling paint on the window behind his chair. "Probably not." Nick answered for her, "You have a nice place here. Why don't I just leave you some brochures? If you find you have some questions you can call us."

"Do you like my place? What do you think of my gardens?"

"Your gardens? Well, I'm no expert on gardens." He glanced around, leaning toward the porch rail. He saw hints, overgrown bushes, and, amidst rotting picket fences and rusting tools, here and there a flash of color. Daylilies, he thought. The wilted ones were irises. He remembered other names from his grandfather's garden. Columbines, or maybe Bleeding Heart. "Nice. Must be a lot of work."

"Oh, they are, but worth it I think. They keep me busy and they give me so much joy." She turned to him again. A faint smile cracked the corners of her fissured lips. They sat silent, the cat between them, its tail raised in a flat S that suggested a cobra about to strike. Nick pretended to write some notes on his clipboard.

"Well, thank you for listening." Nick stood. "I've got quite a few visits to make today."

"Oh, please sit. It's so nice to have a visitor, someone to share my gardens with." She nodded at the chair and Nick sank into it. "I must confess, I was once very selfish, of my garden, I mean. I didn't want to spoil it. I worked so hard at it, you know." Ms. Turner began to tell Nick of her flowers, her vegetables, of how they didn't grow on their own, how they demanded constant attention. How she loved them, the feel of the hard little seeds in her hand, the way they split their husks, pushed through the soil and pointed at the light. Always seeking the light. How they could be directed, shaped and pruned and trained to climb where she wanted them to grow. She described the feeding and watering like a priest explaining a sacrament, her one eye glowing with a banked fire. She discussed disease, blight and mold and the constant threat of pests. She listed insects and birds and mammals and the various countermeasures she employed. Nick listened, glancing restlessly across the property, down at the cat, back to the staring black patch.

"Do you know guns, young man?"

"A little. That looks like a nice one. You don't see too many double barrels anymore." She pushed the gun toward him and he accepted it. He checked the safety first, then pointed it over the railing, gauging the feel. Lowering it, he thumbed the breech lock and snapped it open. He read the numbers circling the brass shell casings. "Twenty gauge, huh? Good choice. Power without too much kick." He wanted to ask why she sat on the porch with a shotgun across her lap. Instead he asked if she hunted.

"No" She laughed. "It's for protection. Do you hunt?"

"Some. Rather unsuccessfully."

"Then you've killed things, animals?"

Nick hesitated. He was way behind schedule, sitting on a crazy lady's porch, holding a loaded shotgun. "Occasionally. Like I said, I'm not a very successful hunter."

"You can shoot, though. You can hit a target?"

"Sure." He shrugged, "I'm a decent shot." He began to hand the gun back to Ms. Turner. She waved it off and turned back to gaze at her yard. Nick could hear birds rustling in the eaves above the porch, and occasionally he caught a glimpse of one flitting by, a twig or bits of grass clenched in its beak. The cat watched, too. It had moved to the edge of the step and twisted its neck upward.

"Look!" Ms. Turner suddenly stood and point across the yard. "There! Do you see it?" Nick rose, too, and tried to follow her finger, but nothing seemed worthy of her excitement. She dropped her voice and commanded him to come. He stood next to her, surprised at how tall she was, and stared down her arm. "You see, he's back! I knew he'd come back. The dirty beast will not leave me alone." She grabbed Nick's arm. "Will you kill him for me?"

"What are you talking about? Kill who?" He began to wiggle his arm gently, trying to break her grip. At first she resisted, but then she let his hand fall.

"The groundhog. He destroys everything. Look at my gardens. I'm too old, too weak, I can't keep up with him. I've tried to kill him. I've tried to ignore him. Nothing works." She laid a hand on Nick's shoulder and stared at him. "Will you? Before he's gone again? You see him don't you. There. By the shed." Nick saw nothing by the shed but the same wild tangle of vegetation that covered her property. Still, he edged a little closer to the rail. "You're a city boy aren't you? You're not used to spotting animals. Do you know what a groundhog looks like? Look closely, now. He hides well, but just wait, he'll move and then you'll see. You'll see."

Nick stared, his eyes raking through the brush, searching for any sign of fur. Nothing. He glanced at the old woman, began to tell her that she was mistaken, but she was staring ahead, holding her breath. Nick studied her patch. It clung to her like desiccated skin, the flesh around it puckered with scars. Nick wondered what the patch hid. He imagined a sunken hole, a tunnel to a dark place. He felt the weight of the gun cradled in his arm, its twin barrels hot with sun. Out at the boundaries of the yard the landscape shimmered.

"I see it." he whispered. He felt her grip tighten on his shoulder. "Yeah, he's a sneaky devil, but I can see him now. Are you sure you want me to shoot him?"

55

Ms. Turner laughed. "Sure? I've been waiting for years for this. Please!" She looked hard at him, then dropped her hand from his shoulder.

"Okay then." Nick shrugged and stepped closer to the railing. He raised the shotgun, tucked it tight into his shoulder and made work of sighting down its twin tapering barrels. He slid the safety up and drew a breath. He heard his father's voice. *Never point a weapon unless you intend to shoot it.* He counted to three in his head and squeezed the trigger.

The gun bucked smart against his shoulder. He turned to Ms. Turner. She stared ahead, a smile creeping across her wizened face. He swung the gun up again, pointed toward the shed, and fired the other barrel. "There. Just to be sure." He cleared the empty shells, laid the open gun in the crook of his arm, and descended the steps. The cat had retreated under a chair at the first blast, but he soon heard it sweeping through the tall, wet grass behind him. He stopped at the shed and poked at the imaginary beast with his foot while the cat traced a figure eight between his legs. Then he turned to the house and called, "It's dead."

Back at the house he handed the emptied gun to Ms. Turner, accepted her tight-lipped thanks, and gathered his clipboard. At the bottom of the steps he turned. "Do you have a shovel? I should bury it."

"Leave it to rot. As a warning." She was already in her chair, the gun comfortable on her lap, her one seeing eye searching.

The boy nodded good-bye and walked from the tired house. As he neared the shed, he stooped to exam the patch of ground he'd targeted. The earth had absorbed both blasts; the overgrown grass had fallen back into place.

He liked that. He meant to do no harm. As he rose he glimpsed the cat stalking, weaving through the broken slats of the picket fence and threading the tangled vegetation. It stopped, and Nick knelt again, peering through the brush, hoping to spot the cat's prey. Instead, he saw a hint of pink, and, reaching in, he touched a flower. He turned toward the house, but it was nearly noon and the old woman had surrendered her post to the sun. Nick set his clipboard down, wrenched open the shed door and retrieved a few rusty tools. He spent the next hour liberating a rose bush, weeding, pruning dead branches, and coaxing budded vines upward until they settled high on the shambled fence. As he walked back to the road, his skin prickled. Someone was watching. He shook his head and kept walking, glancing back just as the driveway turned toward the road. From that distance the old house looked shrunken, its shadowed porch empty, its dark windows blank, like blind eyes staring. The shotgun leaned black and crooked against the wall. *Crazy old woman,* Nick thought.

He turned and headed for the road, kicking at the few loose stones left in the hard-packed drive. Saplings leaned out from under the trees, searching for light. Now and then a car rushed past on the paved road, but mostly Nick listened to the soft sounds of the forest, his foot steps, the tinny ringing in his ears left from the shotgun blasts. He remembered its pleasant weight, the click of the safety, the firm fit of the walnut stock against his shoulder. *Take a breath. Ease it out. Squeeze the trigger.* His father's voice. His father's father's hands on his shoulder, adjusting his stance. Autumns spent standing in his grandfather's garden learning to shoot. A closet full of guns, the smell of oil rags, the green boxes of shells in ranks on the shelves.

Scrapbooks of smiling men in hunting vests, fistfuls of pheasants hanging limp. His grandfather was gone. The guns still stood in the closet, empty barrels pointing up.

He'd parked his car as far off the road as possible, its front bumper almost touched the rusty chain that drooped across the old woman's driveway. Tiger lilies rioted through the road ditches, orange trumpet heads swaying on the end of stiff green stems. Nick stepped over the chain, clicked the button of his remote. He tossed his clipboard on the passenger seat and stood staring at the lilies twitching in the breeze. Then he fished a folding knife from his pocket, cut two flowers—one for each barrel, one for each eye—and began walking back to the house.

Ring of Fire

It was a good night for telling. We'd stopped piling logs on the fire around midnight, dragged our chairs close and sat, positioned like the quarter marks of a clock. Lyle held a bag of marshmallows on his lap, feeding them raw into his mouth, his forgotten roasting stick jammed in the ground. Back then, Sherry and Lyle were still together, but for the group's sake, they kept it low key. A comfortable space divided them, but we all understood which tent they'd share later.

Across from Sherry, Rich nursed a Bud Light; his long legs stretched so close to the fire that I saw steam rising from his sneakers. He was the only one of us close to drunk. It was May, 1991, ten years after we'd graduated high school together. We were a bigger, rowdier bunch in '82, as each passing year college and marriage and the demands of growing up whittled down our numbers. Now, only four of us kept up the tradition.

"Just tell it, man," Rich said. "Nobody gonna hear it but us." He waved his beer-canned hand without looking up from the fire. "We all got stuff we got to get rid of. Tell it. It'll do you good."

It'd taken longer than usual to reach this point of the night. Maybe the unseasonably warm spring fueled our revelry, or maybe we laid extra significance on this tenth anniversary, but we spent most of the night celebrating, staying away from anything too serious. Lyle and Sherry brought T-bones and Rich contributed beer and his mother's homemade rhubarb pie. While they cooked I dragged a dozen wooden pallets from my truck and broke them into firewood. After dinner, Rich and I had stoked the fire until the flames reared up taller than us, spitting spirals of embers and smoke into a starless night. I opened my truck doors, popped cassettes into the deck and cranked Jackson Browne and Springsteen. Lyle and Sherry danced, the wild glare of the fire making their shadows climb the dark trees. Rich tried his best to distract me by tossing a football around, but I kept forgetting to toss it back. I lost my vision in the fire and bobbled the ball in its unpredictable light.

Still later, we'd chased through the dark woods, shouting and shrieking like kids. We played flashlight tag, until Rich claimed he'd spotted a skunk. Then, regrouped around the fire, Lyle shared coffee from his battered thermos. I unpacked the marshmallows and chocolate bars and we sat whittling points on sticks and waiting for the fire to burn down to a more manageable heat.

The night slipped in around us. For a while at least, we fought it with loud talk and laughter, but finally we let it settle over us and submitted. Listened. Listened while frogs drummed and the fire snapped and the breeze played the trees. No one spoke because our words sounded foreign here.

If it weren't for the bugs, we might have sat silent all night. But they winged in out of the dark, a clumsy invasion of large beetles drawn to the fire. Some bumped stupidly against our backs and fell hard to the earth. Grounded, they resumed their pilgrimage, their bronze shells metallic in the fire light. Others were caught in the fire's draft and disappeared in the flames, shooting straight up with the rising smoke. You couldn't help but feel sorry for them, but it was funny, too. Rich grabbed a stick, yelled "Batter up" and swung away at the bugs. Sherry laughed and tossed her head, using her long red pony tail to sweep June bugs from her back. I've never seen anything like it since.

After a while Rich began reminiscing about our first camping trip. It was a worn old story, and we quickly moved on to the present, griping about work, catching up on family and old friends. "Did you see Jimmy's dad in the paper?" Lyle asked, "They interviewed him about the war. Said Jimmy was in the first wave out of Kuwait."

"Crazy stuff." Rich said. "Plowed over those trenches with bulldozer blades. Buried the Iraqis alive. All that hype about Saddam's Republican Guard and then we squash 'em like bugs."

Lyle laughed. "Alright, alright, I've got a confession. Back in college I got smart, swore I'd never vote Republican. So last election, it's Bush or Dukakis. Guess what? I can't vote for Dukakis. I surely can't vote Republican." He shoved another marshmallow in his mouth and chewed.

"Tell it." Rich demanded.

"Nothing to tell. Voted for Dukakis anyway. Didn't matter a bit. He lost. We got Bush and a quick little war." He picked up a slab of wood and tossed it in the fire. "Maybe it's all okay. War's over. Hail to the chief. Wave the flag and wait."

Sherry snorted. "Wait. Wave the flag and wait. That's all we're supposed to do. You ever hear of Vietnam? How about Grenada? Remember the marines in Lebanon . . ."

"Screw the history lesson, Sherry." Rich stood and glared through the fire. "Sometimes it's necessary. Sometimes ya have to take the bad guy out."

"And sometimes you're just the bad guy."

They went on like that, tossing tired positions back and forth, Sherry batting back Rich's AM talk radio arguments, grinning over the ease of it. Lyle finally stood, looking from one to the other. Come on, man, I thought, say something. Take a side. But after an awkward pause, he just sat down. It worked anyway, I guess. They shut up and we stared into the fire, poking at it with our sticks. The old pallets burned fast, turned quickly to coals. Flames shimmered like silver ghosts guarding the embers.

"I have a confession." I said.

"Just tell it, man," Rich said. "Nobody gonna hear it but us all." He pronounced it like a true gospel preacher.

And so I did. Maybe I was thinking about lost opportunities, about things that seemed too big to stop. Maybe I just wanted a reaction. For whatever reason, I told them about my dad and my sister Katie. And then I told what I never did about it. It wasn't everything. I didn't *know* everything, couldn't or wouldn't remember it all, but I hoped it was enough. I didn't make anything up or intentionally leave anything out, but can't deny that I told it for effect. Head down, speaking the words into the fire. That worked, too, I guess. Nobody had anything to say.

Finally, I heard Rich lift the cooler lid and fish a can from the ice. He pulled the tab and drank. "It was a long time ago, man. You were just a kid. What the hell were you gonna do anyway?" Out of the corner of my eye I watched him lean forward, his head between his knees. Across the fire Lyle sighed.

"How is Katie?" Lyle asked. "Married, right?"

"Married. Two kids, another coming." I answered. "Doing great, really. Loves Oregon. Husband's cool." I looked over at Sherry.

She stared at me, her back pillared, her chin up. She sat low on an old canvas camp stool, the folding kind that opens so the legs form an X. Her feet were propped on a log and she held her knees tight, hands clamped in fists on them. I looked away and bent my head to the fire, waiting for her to say something. Instead, she stood up and marched off into the dark. Lyle swore toward us and hurried after her, calling her name softly.

After a few more minutes I said goodnight to Rich, unrolled my sleeping bag in the back of the old truck and stretched a tarp over the bed. When I laid down my feet pushed against the cab wall, and the snug posture brought some small comfort as I listened to the night. Later I heard Sherry and Lyle shuffle past, whispering, then the slow and deliberate sound of their tent fly zipping up. Back down.

Sherry shook me awake some time before dawn. She was bending down next to the tailgate when I opened my eyes. Her face was inches from mine.

"Sorry," she whispered. "I couldn't sleep." She stood and held the tarp up as I wiggled out. We sat on the edge of the tailgate. I crossed my arms against the cool, damp air. Sherry slid closer.

"I keep thinking about Katie. She was so pretty and . . . I don't know . . . graceful, I guess. Someone to look up to. I can't believe it. "

I rubbed my eyes and shrugged, working the stiffness out of my neck. Sherry smelled warm, like all bodies do after sleeping. "Remember the Fourth of July parades? She

63

used to ride in the back of this truck, all star-spangled, waving and smiling like a pageant queen. Your dad's *personal* pageant queen. Can't believe I was jealous."

Through the trees, patches of charcoal sky lightened, then began to glow like fanned coals. Sherry wrapped her arms across her chest and shivered. "You should've told me. It should kill us to keep that inside, but we all do it, don't we? Pretend. Wait for someone else to take a stand." She turned toward me. "It's not too late. You should do something. I don't know what, something to let him know you know. So he doesn't just get away with it." She laid her hand on mine. "You still could. You still *should*." She squeezed my hand. When it was almost light she slid off the tailgate and walked to the fire. I watched her crouch there, pick up a stick, and prod the gray coals, stirring them back to life, muttering *should* as she stabbed a few into crumbs.

Two weeks later, the Saturday before Memorial Day, my dad called from Arizona. He reminded me to take a grass clipper to the cemetery and tidy up around Uncle Pete's grave. "Sweep the clipping off the headstone. You know those lazy city workers. Pick up a flag, just in case. Doubt if they'll forget this year, though. Everyone's a patriot after we win a war." His sarcastic sneer squeezed through the phone. "Hey, I've been thinking. What if you drove the truck in the parade? Dress it up nice, like we used to do. Remember the bicentennial? She looked good then. Just a suggestion." With my father there are no suggestions.

"I'll think about it." I said.

"Good. Don't forget Uncle Pete's grave. Wouldn't hurt to call us once and a while, either. Even better, come and visit. Your mother misses you."

I made some vague assurance and changed the subject. His mission accomplished, my dad half-muttered a good-bye and handed the phone to my mom.

Dad. He worked forty years for a local office-furniture maker. Every Saturday he spent hours washing the truck and our family car by hand. Each summer he pitched for two fast-pitch softball teams. His garden was the biggest, most productive, and he proudly shared his surplus with our less successful neighbors. If a neighbor kid's bike squeaked, my dad oiled it. He put up a basketball hoop and organized us into teams, calling double dribbles and correcting our shots. If we fought, he sent somebody home. Every Saturday, at 2:00 p.m. he went to the barber. On Sunday, we sat in the front pew. We were never late.

The truck has been in our family longer than me. A 1958 Ford F-150, my dad bought it new, two months after my sister was born. He never bought another new vehicle until he retired at age sixty.

I can't remember a Fourth of July without my dad's tradition of decorating the old truck for the Independence Day parade. Red, with a white band that ran along the top of the cargo bed and up the cab roof, it fit perfectly among all the fire trucks and vintage tractors. Starting at dawn the day of the parade, Mom and Dad would decorate it with red, white and blue streamers and pompoms. Dad would fasten tiny flags to the bumpers, front and back. And me, I rode in it, at least until I was old enough to decorate my bike and join the rest of the kids just behind the fire trucks.

When Katie turned twelve, Dad decided she would ride in the back. Mom sewed her a red and white blouse and a blue pleated skirt. Dad made a custom stool at work, one that bolted to the truck bed. It had a red cushion that swiveled on bearings so Katie could sit and turn from side to side. Dad called it Katie's throne. He said she had a fine parade wave. I never saw her wave, but I saw pictures thanks to mom, who would stake a claim early, parked in her aluminum lawn chair with the Kodak and the Super 8. It was a fine parade wave.

I called Katie on Memorial Day. Gideon, her oldest, answered. She wasn't home. "Tell your mom that Grandpa wants me to drive the truck in the parade. Try not to forget, okay." Gideon promised to pass the message along. I didn't really expect a call.

Her letter arrived on Friday. She'd scrawled a quick update on spring green stationary. One of the kids had decorated it with crayoned flowers. She made no mention of my message, just tucked a yellowed newspaper clipping in the envelope. It was a picture of her waving from the back of the truck. Little Katie, smiling boldly into the lens. She'd taped a snapshot to the back of the clipping. In it my dad stands in the back of the truck, his hairy arms draped over Katie's shoulder. He's smiling broadly. Katie is older in that picture and pretty as ever. She's leaning away from my dad, her face turned to the side, her eyes hidden. I'd never seen the picture before. I sat, flipping the two images back and forth, surprised my sister kept them.

There was one more photo in the envelope. Katie's curled on a couch, smiling down at Gideon and Lisa. The kids sit in a sea of crumpled wrapping paper, caught in the act of gift-opening. Her husband Rob leans awkwardly from the corner, his clowning face smiling, unsure if he'd officially made it into the shot after setting the timer. Everything is a little out of focus. The kids are still in their pajamas and Katie's hair is rumpled, her smiling eyes still weighted with sleep. Only Rob seems to notice the camera.

A few weeks later I bumped into Sherry at the grocery store. Right away she started asking me about Katie.

"She's doing great," I said, "I just got a letter from her. Talked all about her kids, even sent a picture of them at Christmas."

"That's great. I'm glad she stays in touch."

"Well, I called her first," I laughed, "Then she sent the letter."

"What a good little brother. I can't remember the last time my brother called me." Sherry reached across me to grab a box of Cheerios. She put the box in her cart and stepped closer.

"I called to ask her about the parade. My dad wants me to drive the truck in the parade."

"Really. What'd she say?"

"Nothing." I shrugged. "Not sure what to do. What do you think?"

"Seriously? Why give him the satisfaction? Screw that old truck."

"Yeah. That's what I was thinking, too." We pushed to the end of the aisle together.

"Well, I blew my budget. I'll see you around." She brushed my cheek with a kiss. "Screw that damn truck." She said. Then she pushed off toward the check out lanes.

For a few days I thought I would follow her advice, but as the parade entry deadline loomed, I found myself in line at city hall, filling out the appropriate paperwork. The last week of June, I drove to Pam's Party Central. I stood in the aisle, stymied by all the patriotic extravagance. Besides all the stars and stripes and the omnipresent spirit of 1776 signs there were flags honoring Desert Storm, flags emblazoned with M1 tanks and F16 fighter jets. Celebrating independence by taking down a tyrant.

Still, I didn't ignore Sherry. I daydreamed all kinds of dark, vengeful fantasies about the truck and the parade. I snapped out of these dreams to a fading image of a bolder and more reckless image of myself stopped in the middle of the route and, with everyone watching, smashing the truck with a sledge hammer. I thought of spray painting obscenities in black on the sides. I looked into renting a PA system and blasting hardcore punk. In the end I figured I didn't have the guts for anything so dramatic.

Coming home from work one day I took a short cut through the mall. The Sears store had recently closed. Discarded store fixtures cluttered the parking lot around three stuffed dumpsters. Poking around, I spotted a plastic hand, chipped and upturned, reaching from under a pile of water-stained pegboard. I gripped it and tugged. The hand belonged to a battered mannequin. One arm was broken off at the elbow. She stared off vacantly, her plastic smile permanent and beguiling. I picked her up and slid her into the back of my truck. There was nothing complicated about her. Her arms swiveled at the shoulder. Her waist bent into a seated pose. I slammed the tailgate in place and drove home, listening to her slide around behind me.

For two days I lived with a mannequin in my apartment. I set her across from me at my tiny kitchenette. She smiled pleasantly while I ate and read the paper. She greeted me unclothed and shameless when I returned from church on Sunday morning. I spent the rest of the day studying her. She didn't mind my staring.

Just before going to bed that night, I grabbed a black permanent marker and, starting in the middle of her forehead, drew a line down, dividing her in half. The line traced over her gently upturned nose and her pale pink lips, down her long neck and through the valley between her slight and rounded breasts. I stopped just north of her navel. Then I opened my pocket knife and hacked one side of her head free of its synthetic blond hair. After that, I went to bed.

Monday night I bought paints and brushes and set to work. I painted half of her, the half with the intact arm, blue from the waist down, and striped her face and torso red and white. The other half of her I covered in flat black, except for the eye, which I circled in a sick yellow-green. I left the hand flesh-colored, painting each nail red or blue. The middle finger nail I painted black.

Tuesday night I worked under the parking lot lights, determining how to secure a kitchen stool to the truck floor. My solution, a twisted mess of baling wire, would have made my father cringe. Then, back in my apartment, I practiced strapping the mannequin to the stool. As a final touch, I reconfigured a dozen miniature flags, reversing them so they hung upside down on their staffs.

Wednesday night I called Rich and asked if I could borrow his garage. He stood watching me while I rigged the mannequin in place, positioning flags and taping white and blue streamers to the truck. He sipped a beer and shook his head. "You're nuts, man," he said and left me to finish alone. Before I turned in, I called Sherry. She didn't answer, so I left her a message, expressing my hopes that she would go to the parade in the morning.

69

Thursday, the Fourth, I jogged to Rich's house in a muggy drizzle. He was waiting for me in the garage. "Now what?" he asked, handing me a cup of a coffee.

I shrugged. "Not sure. I wasn't planning on rain. The paint will probably run before I even get in line."

"Yeah. Figured that." Rich set his coffee down and rummaged through some boxes. "Here," he handed me a roll of plastic. "Wrap her in this. At least she'll stay dry till you get there. Maybe it'll clear up." He rolled up the overhead door and leaned outside, looking west. "I probably *won't* come and watch."

I wrapped the opaque plastic around her, fastening it to the floor with duct tape. Then I drove slowly to the staging area, watching the plastic snap like a tattered sail in my rear view mirror. I arrived late, but this was no problem, as the rain had slowed everything down. We formed a damp and zigzagging line in the high school parking lot. Cops, glowering under their plastic-wrapped brims, stopped traffic and waved the parade forward. Striking up a patriotic march, the band swung into the street. Boy Scouts and gray-haired veterans led, followed by a National Guard 6 x 6 pulling a small howitzer. The line snaked forward.

The sky lightened. My windshield wipers squeaked across dry glass. Switching them off, I stomped on the emergency brake and jumped out of the truck. I tugged the plastic loose from the truck floor and tucked a corner of it between the box and the cab. Then, with a parade volunteer waving me forward, I jumped back in the cab and turned into the street.

Despite the rain, a good crowd lined both sides of the street. People folded umbrellas and shook off hats and hoisted toddlers on shoulders. I watched the roof of the convertible Mustang in front of me as it accordioned up and back. Two pretty blondes climbed on top of the rear seat and began tossing candy excitedly. The crowd laughed and cheered. Nobody seemed very interested in my plastic-wrapped cargo.

I waited. The sun warmed the cab and I cranked the window down. In spite of the thumping drums and occasional siren, I could hear the plastic rattling behind me. Loosened, it lifted and fluttered over the mannequin. I stared straight ahead, concentrating on the Mustang's brake lights. They flickered off and on, marking the staccato progress of the parade. Each time we stopped, the plastic would float down, settling like a discarded shroud. I imagined my mom in her chair, the camera humming in her hand, trying to figure out what was under the plastic. Wondering where Katie was.

We crawled down Main Street, through our fading business district, then turned right past city hall. Store fronts gave over to houses. I stuck my hand out the window and tried waving like my dad always did. People watched from chairs and blankets on their lawns. I caught a few puzzled stares, but for the most part, no one noticed. I shrugged it off—who wouldn't rather watch two pretty girls throw candy from a convertible? Sherry's parents lived a few blocks down. I figured that if she was watching, it would be along this stretch. I waited one more block and when the line stalled again I stuck my hand through the window, grabbed the corner of the plastic and tugged.

It slid easy at first, then snagged. I yanked it a few times, then set the brake and leaned out the window. Bunching the damp plastic sheeting with both hands, I jerked hard. Something gave and I almost fell. I wrapped the plastic into a ball and pulled it through the window. Someone honked. I released the brake and lurched forward. In the mirror, I saw the mannequin listing toward the driver's side, paint still intact. My face reddened.

I leaned into the breeze to cool my flushing face. In the side mirror I watched a boy dash into the street and pick something up. He lifted it, black and crooked, above his head and waved it at me. "Hey," he yelled, "Hey, mister." Then he ran up to my window and handed me the mannequin's arm.

I took the offered arm and thanked the kid. He didn't say anything, just stood staring at the back of the truck. The line started again. I looked ahead and saw the Mustang pulling away. One of the girls riding in the back yelled something to the kid. Then they all laughed. I tossed the arm on the seat and jammed the truck into gear.

I took the next right, breaking ranks and hurrying away from the parade. The mannequin rode tilted and armless behind me, tapping against the cab window with every bump in the road. Now we drove through flag-festooned streets. Muggy air swirled through the window, scented here and there with charcoal smoke. I heard the *snap-pop-pop-pop* of kids playing with firecrackers, and pushed a cassette into the deck.

Somehow, I ended up behind the emptied Sears store. There was only one dumpster left. I parked behind it and climbed into the back of the truck. The mannequin tipped her face up at me, still smiling. I grabbed her by the shoulders, propping her straight. Then I stood back and kicked. I kicked until she hung from the side of the stool, her half arm propping her against the floor. I kicked at the stool until the legs bent and my feet ached. Finally I grabbed the seat and twisted, back and forth, growling

72

through gritted teeth. The wires that bound the stool to the truck bed snapped. I hurled the stool and the mannequin over the side of the dumpster. It landed with a dull metallic clatter. Then I circled the truck, stripping the last of the flags and streamers, and tossing them blindly over the dumpster's wall. The last thing I threw in was the wadded plastic.

At home I dragged my TV out on my tiny balcony and watched the Tigers trample Boston 6 – 1. Below me screaming little kids chased each other with squirt guns and water balloons while adults lined up picnic tables in the yellow grass. Somewhere among the identical balconies a tape player kept repeating R.E.M.'s *Losing my Religion*. Repeat and rewind. Repeat and rewind. Repeat. I listened, remembering Sherry telling me once that the song wasn't about religion at all. Instead, it had something to do with obsessive love.

Just before dark I drove to a gas station and paid a deposit on a borrowed five gallon gas can. I drove back to the mall and parked next to the Sears dumpster. Leaning over the side, I doused everything with gasoline. I tossed a match. The gasoline ignited with a hollow *whump*. Smoke roiled up black into the night like a campfire. I sat alone on the hood of my truck and watched the town's fireworks arc up and explode over the mall roof. After the grand finale, I climbed back up and peeked over the side. She lay in a puddle of melted plastic, charred but intact. Apparently five gallons of regular wasn't enough.

I told Rich that a few days later, after I picked up a new roll of plastic at the hardware store. "No?" He said "Not enough for who?"

"To burn the thing." Then I caught his question. "For Katie."

"Oh yeah. Katie." Rich laughed a little. "I forgot about Katie. Sorta thought the whole thing might have been about impressing Sherry." He looked down at the floor. "Either way, Katie or Sherry, you're right. You'll never do enough." And after all is said and done, I think he's probably right.

Our tenth anniversary camping trip was the last. A while back Sherry moved to Denver. As far as I know, Lyle's still trying to figure out an excuse that will make his following her seem less like stalking. Rich still camps, but now it's with his wife and kids.

This spring, I'm flying to Portland to see Gideon graduate from high school. He's thinking about the Marines, wishes he could have been in Baghdad when they pulled down Saddam's statue. I hope to talk him out of it. Toppled statues and burnt mannequins. Read what you want into them, but symbols, like motives, only go so far.

I'm staying a few days after my folks fly back to my father's beloved Arizona desert. Katie says I should just stay in Oregon for good. She keeps telling me how safe and peaceful she feels falling asleep every night surrounded by mountains.

Straight and Plumb, Square and True

In those days they were giants, men of renown,
shapers of wood and brick and iron. The boy peered up at
the towering, beam-shouldered men, stern faces sun-baked
and wind-reddened, entering the store in booted strides.
They extended calloused hands to his father, joked and
complained. When enough was enough, they got down to
business reciting the day's needs from lists scrawled on
scraps of pine trim or penciled on tiny spiral-bound note
pads. To the boy, their words rang cryptic and veiled, a
language further masked by each speaker's peculiar
rendering.

But his father—by necessity a master of translation—
nodded knowingly, and, threading narrow aisles, weighed
nails, counted carriage bolts and offered advice. Most of
the men left the boy alone. Some nodded dismissively. A
few bothered to know his name. He stood broom in hand,
watching each exchange with a certain fearsome awe. He
did not like most of them, but could not resist the urge to
admire all of them. They were, it seemed, men who knew
all necessary things. Skilled with nearly all of the neatly
pegged and shelved tools in the store, they built buildings,
housed working class and wealthy alike. Applying the
principles of plumb and square with doctrinal clarity to all
things, they clothed themselves with confidence. Still,
what impressed the boy more than the carpenters' skills, or
even their towering presence was the way his father dealt
with them. For, in the boy's mind, his father was a great

man, the greatest man he knew. Yet, before these men, he willingly stepped into their shadows.

When the boy watched the carpenters wrap their mighty hands around his father's, or pluck a pencil stub from behind an ear, he sensed their power. Power of muscle and sinew sheathed in calloused and scarred flesh —but more than that. Theirs were hands that knew. More than grasping apparatuses, not mere extensions of something, not even a symbol, but the very center of their existence. It occurred to the boy that the rest of their bodies—their strong backs and bending knees, their roped arms and barrel chests—were secondary. He saw this best in a few old carpenters whose bibbed overalls dangled from their shrinking frames. These were men whose hips and knees had long ago frozen like rusted iron, yet their hands refused to slow. Even the mind, the boy thought, was only as good as the parts it commanded. In fact, watching, he wondered if the great hands, the ones that did what others could not, had minds of their own. At some point, then, he became to believe and to believe firmly that it was a man's hands and what he could do with them that distinguished one from another.

The summer of his sixteenth year, the boy graduated from the backroom to the sales floor. Shy but determined, he wandered the aisles, stocking shelves, watching the door, mapping every corner. absorbing the store in its entirety. He already knew what things were and how they worked, and he did well with the old ladies and younger customers, the neighborhood folks who needed hose washers and furnace filters, light bulbs and mops. At first, he shrank from the builders and they responded in kind. A few, men who found in his father both a friend and a shopkeeper, offered him simple tasks. He earned some respect. He blundered. He winced and endured their ribbing. Following in their shadows and listening, laughing at jokes he didn't understand, he gleaned scraps of truth. From these scraps he assembled a creed of his own, *Praise is earned, not gifted. Boasting is only for joking. Good workmanship is the truest language. Humility is unspoken. Anger is reserved for those you trust, never waste it on fools. A man's word is his honor. A hand shake carries the weight of a signed document.* With the creed came confidence, and soon he found himself asking the occasional question. Sometimes the mighty men lowered their faces and answered.

The boy had learned young that his hands were adequate. Sickly and protected, he spent hours modeling houses and locomotives and trucks that soon gave way to a whole miniature world surrounded by circling trains. His fingers followed his mind's command until, practiced, they cut and shaped and assembled things without conscious instruction. His father took notice, admiring. He gave his son bigger challenges and tools fit for the scale of the work. His first attempt, a pine jewelry box for Mothers Day, he smashed to kindling when the lid failed to fit. The rest—an oak serving tray, a birdfeeder, a set of book ends—he presented to his father, who studied them with keen eye and tilted head. Laying his hand on the boy's boney shoulders, he would assess the sum of it, noting the worthy and leaving the rest unsaid. But the boy heard the unsaid and came to see his flaws. And in this way he learned. He built a bluebird house, a garden shed, and, finally, a sturdy pantry cabinet. He discovered the necessary truth of square edges and straight lines, the value of lumber and labor, that mistakes could be fixed, and that craftsmanship could cover flaws. He began to understand something of the men he esteemed.

Then he went to work among them. He earned a wage driving nails under the watchful and sparse-worded tutelage of three aging brothers. All three of them, Lawrence, Ray, and Jack, would address him by last name only and say, "Like this," as their hands flashed, measuring and marking, their forearms baptized by saw dust, their eyes fixed on the work. Then he followed their form, waiting for some acknowledgment, a nod, a rarely spoken "Good." They valued one way for every task—*their* way to stack lumber, to hold a broom, to plumb a door jamb. The boy supposed there were other ways practiced by other men, but he kept that to himself. There were times he stopped working to watch them, to marvel at these men who straightened bent nails, men whose toolboxes still held brace drills and handsaws. He was content to breathe their exhalations.

Always precisely at noon, work paused and they assembled for lunch. The brothers talked politics and doctrine and assessed the declining condition of the world. They held strong and parallel opinions, but always managed to find points of contention. Each day, by the time the boy finished his first sandwich, the positions had been staked. Good-natured but serious, the brothers battled gamely until, by carefully mapped but circuitous routes, they ended at some point of agreement. Often Ray played the role of mediator, drawing a common line between the contenders until, at the exact appointed time, the three closed their emptied lunch boxes and returned to work. One task set aside for another. To the boy, this too was a mystery.

At night, the boy returned to his father's table. Unleashed from the silence of the day, he spoke of work and all he had learned. His parents listened and nodded, smiling at each other across steaming potatoes. With dinner cleared and the Bible read, he would leave to meet his girl and start all over. She too, listened. Letting him tell her all of the ideas he assembled and boxed while pounding twelve-penny nails, driving hundreds of pair plate to stud. Finally, spent of words, he would find his hand wrapped in hers. Her fingers traced tiny orbits over his hardening calluses until he finally remembered to ask about her day. When she spoke it was with fewer words, truer words somehow.

He worked three years with the old carpenters. When he left them to return to his father's shop, he thought that through them he had learned everything about building and much about life. He could judge the better of two vacant lots and proceed to locate the best place to site the house. He could scribe a cabinet flush to a crooked wall. He understood the language: *straight* and *plumb* and *square* and *true*. Understood that behind these words hid something deeper than language. The old men taught him, too, about loyalty—it was nearly everything—and honesty and keeping promises, especially costly ones. They abhorred both bankruptcy and divorce, seeing them as varying degrees of the same vile sin. At times, their hearts also wore calluses. This was one thing the boy knew but did not know, could not have consciously admitted.

He was afraid to tell them he was leaving. The night before he did so, though, the girl held his hand and asked "Are you sure?" and when he nodded, she said, "Then tell them. They'll understand. They'll respect you." They did both, shaking his hands and blessing them.

He returned to his father's shop and married the girl the following June. And, according to her carefully determined calendar and the mystery of nature, their first child, a boy, was born three years later. A girl and then another followed. Three faces smiling in the window when he returned home, three sets of little hands wrapping his legs.

He built his father's business by applying his firsthand knowledge of his customers' language to the store's advantage. Each night he returned home to her table, to crayoned colored gifts, to toy layered floors, to their bed. Late at night, he rolled the old rules through his head, testing each day against them.

At first, when the old carpenters began to fail, he was too busy chasing the next generation of builders to notice. They were memories, faces staring from old black and white photos tacked to the office wall, names on yellowed and hand-scrawled invoices. Occasionally he saw them in church and around town, their gait stiff and bent, overworked joints rebelling. Their ears were dulled by the harsh whine of power saws and he raised his voice to banter with them, checking for the old spark, the pride and determination that marked them. The spark was there, but their intensity banked. He missed their bullheaded sparring, even their unreasonable expectations. The new breed—loafer-shod number crunchers and crude wood butchers—disappointed him. The gentlemen, the giants, were all dead or retired.

When the brothers themselves began to die, it shook him. Lung cancer took Ray first. Lawrence followed suit four years later. They had faded to a comfortable story in his mind, a legend he shared with his children and the young clerks at the store. They were the mightiest of the mighty to him, not in physical strength but in what they knew. He built a world of surety around their memory. Stubborn and determined, always testing the new, they followed their old ways until one by one they retired. Busy with his own life, their decline surprised him. He visited a few times, listening to stories of sickness and enfeebled wives, children who spurned their teachings and those who remained loyal. He fancied himself one of the latter, a keeper of their philosophy. Travel and circumstance prevented him from attending the funerals of Lawrence and Ray. In some small and shameful way, he was relieved.

When the last brother passed, his wife insisted that they would not stay away. She took his hand and led him to the car, then gripped it again as they climbed the steps to the funeral chapel. Arriving late, they stood side by side as the line snaked torturously forward, his wife acting as his voice when, overwhelmed, he stumbled over names and failed at conversation. He barely addressed the widow, his hands swallowing hers, his eyes moist with memory. The old man lay in rigid repose, face lined by a lifetime of sun and wind, the corners of his eyes drawn in permanent squint. He looked so formal without a hat. Across his hollowed frame, his hands gathered, his mighty right overlapping the left. He studied the carpenter's hands, as if unfolded they might still reveal something hidden. He felt a tug on his own hand, and turned to find his wife's eyes coaxing him back. The widow slid off her stool and walked, bent but sure, to the casket. Leaning forward, she kissed her husband's forehead, her hand resting gently on his. As he considered all of this, lips on waxen flesh, the widow's soft caress, the stiff, frozen hands, the tough old body displayed in plush upholstery, the man felt his wife's hand mimic the widow's. Calm, they slipped away, past the grey-suited man holding the door, into the dusk-dimmed night.

Outside they paused. To the west the sun had moved on, leaving the sky above the distant trees blazing, extravagant, opaque with hallowed fire. They stood, watching the colors seep into the dark. Behind them the moon rose full and reverent. A car door slammed shut, and he looked away from the sky. A young couple walked hand in hand across the quiet parking lot. They whispered between each other, stopping for a moment at a set of low concrete steps while the young woman shifted her purse and straightened her man's collar. Then she took his hand and they climbed the steps, her heels ringing hammer-hard. The older couple stepped aside as they passed, and the man recognized the boy, who nodded a nervous greeting. He was the son of a customer, following his father into the trades. The older man tried to nod back some kind of assurance but it was lost in the dim light. He stood in the damp grass next to his wife, and they waited until the young couple climbed the next set of steps and slipped through the door of the funeral home. The door swung shut and they were alone again in the quiet. "Coffee?" he asked, "Pie?" She smiled. They slipped toward the parking lot, their steps muffled in the silent summer grass.

Still Born

In the beginning there is a door. I'll concede that much. A door of flesh that does not hinge so much as it dilates, but an opening, nonetheless, and we all pass through. That is about where the comparison ends. We don't really *know* much about what's behind the door. Sure, we *know,* from the outside. Obstetricians will argue that science—with its sonograms and dissections—offers a view, but none of us *remember* that small and muffled place; none of us can describe the journey down the birth canal, the first flash of light in our clouded eyes, the shadow of our mother's scissored legs (how often I forget that you, my dear child, knew none of these). No one can conjure the feeling of the first touch of hands—loving, nervous, indifferent or divine—that broke our fall. Our first remembered thoughts begin months, even years later. We simply *believe* it happened because we are here and somebody told us and if we are brave and privileged enough we have witnessed it ourselves. But really, what happens behind that door is a mystery rivaled only by death.

Still, if the ending must mirror the beginning, if you insist on a door to exit through, then make it be like the first one, without hinges or locks or choice. Who—except the weary and the sick—would stand patiently and knock? So when folks talk about death's door, I tell your brother to laugh at them. I don't want him to be rude, but sometimes ignorance demands it. Scripture dislikes scoffers, but it also condemns fools.

Instead of a door I imagine a slope, a hill whose summit is birth. Who hasn't heard the expression "It's all down hill from here?" A stupid joke, emblazoned on cheap party hats and little black cocktail napkins, associated with milestone birthdays of forty and fifty. It assumes the existence of a counter-position, an upward climb and a plateau—the fabled prime-of-life—before the descent. But what of you? What of lives cut short on the incline, long before the promised peak? Or those whose path is forever blind groping, stumbling stubbed-toed and twisted-ankled, two sliding steps backward for every one scrambled forward. What kind of ascent is that? For you, my dear one, there was not even a breath, much less a step. Without even opening your eyes, you tumbled away.

○

He is sure the car was green. A forest green wagon, a Ford maybe, a Falcon with those big round taillights that blaze like jet engines. The only pictures are black and white. It doesn't matter. Memories form inside, on the long bench seat where he sits propped against his mother. It is summer and hot and his skinny legs stick to the vinyl. His toes point up at the edge of the seat. Saddle shoes, maybe. He's not sure. Beside him, his mother's purse is a shiny taupe wall. He looks up. She stares, intent over the huge steering wheel, cranks the window open an inch or two. The wind grabs her scarf-wrapped hair. Scowling, she adjusts the window up until the pinched opening emits an angry whistle. She glances down, squeezes out a smile, pats his scraped knees. Then her eyes seize the road again.

The rest he is unsure of. He remembers turning, the crunch of gravel under tires. His mother drives slowly, almost stopping several times. She rolls her window all the way down and leans her head out. Still the car rolls forward. He can't see. He scoots to the edge of the big seat, presses his hand against the hot dash. Without looking, his mother slides him back against the seat. "Wait." she says, "We're almost there." Then she jabs the brake hard. If it weren't for her hand against his chest, he would slide off the seat.

"This is it." She sighs and looks down at him. Sweat-damp curls bracket her green eyes. "Now wait. I'll be just a minute. You're being such a good boy." She pushes the door open, steps out, straightens her skirt at the waist. "I'll be back. Watch me." Then she opens the back door and removes a green bucket, gripping it by its arching metal handle. The bucket is filled with flowers. He sits on his knees at his mother's window and watches her heft the bucket across the grass. She stops just short of the main road and sets its down. Then she slips her hem just above her knees and kneels.

The boy watches the road, the rushing trucks belching smoke as they mount the hill, the slick gleam of cars flashing in the afternoon sun. Two robins chase each other. His mother stands, pushes down on the bucket, twisting so it sits level. Then she bends and brushes the overgrown grass, her fingers sweeping it from side to side. In a minute she is back at the car, smiling at the boy. "You were so good, so patient. Thank you." She drives without talking, turns the radio off, stares ahead.

That's all he remembers. A car ride with his mother. A bucket of flowers. A wide expanse of yellowed turf. For years he never thinks of it.

Did they take other trips? He doesn't remember. He remembers long summer drives to the country, falling asleep on his father's leg as *the* Ernie Harwell called Tigers baseball over the radio. He remembers driving with his mother every Saturday to buy groceries, or, when he was older, to the doctor every Wednesday for allergy shots. He remembers tracing his name on fogged windows, bracing for icy road stops, sitting backward in the rear-facing seat with his big sister. But that trip, with the flowers in the back and the look on his mother's face. It stands out. Vivid like the colored scenes from the *Wizard of Oz.* Hot asphalt, oiled gravel, burnt diesel and his mother's sweat. Does he really remember that? Did any of it happen? Or does he just need it to be real?

○

When your little brother was born we were flooded with cards and celebration. Your mother packed them in a hat box, or something like one, and treasured them. The box sat in a second floor bedroom closet, a room that might have been yours one day.

These celebratory cards shared a shelf with another box filled with cards of consolations and shared grief, cards about you. One afternoon, before the girls came home from school, we sat at the kitchen table and read each one. We cried, then we packed them away. As far as I can remember—and my memory slips here, too—we never consulted either box. We just kept them. When we sold the house and moved, we packed them and took them along, but I would forget them until searching for something, I'd push a picnic basket or an old crock pot out of the way and there they'd sit, side by side. Siblings. Even then I left them alone, especially yours. Like the Ark of the Covenant, one knew to keep at a reverent distance. The box of cards was more than a receptacle, more than a symbol, and we circled it with fearful awe. I tried to tell her, as though I had arrived at a discovery, that there was more than pain in that box. She set her face and stared back at me and said, "I know that." You never saw that face, I know. If you had, you would fall silent, too. (But that is exactly how you fell.)

Now, though, I'm sure others have found those boxes, unless your mother committed one final act of suppression and destroyed them—destroyed your box at least. But I doubt it. She found great comfort and balance in the two of them side by side. Maybe without the one there is no need for the other.

○

When the boy was grown he forgot. He forgot the car ride and the grassy place and the green bucket. He forgot the box of cards he found once when he was scouting for hidden Christmas gifts. He forgot that it was grey and six-sided and that the cover fit snuggly over an inner lip so that when he closed it again it sighed and resisted. The cards inside were smaller than the birthday cards he received every year. The predominant color scheme was blue, soft baby blues and whites turning toward yellow and, at the center, darker indigo-inked messages with exclamation points. He read a few with the vague curiosity of a child tiptoeing into the guarded world of adults, but he quit before he understood. The other box, the sad one, evaded his discovery.

That he had another sister was not forgotten, but the fact wasn't exactly discussed either. She was "The Baby We Lost." For a while he thought of her as a missing child. *Why aren't we looking for her?* He was too young for euphemisms. In fact, she *was* a lost child, lost from the family history, lost from his story. Sometimes he tried to miss her, to mourn for her like he thought he should, but like the box of cards, he couldn't understand what it meant.

○

Forgive me, little one. I've wandered off topic. I was talking about a slope and I mean to continue. Since you are my one and only intended audience, it can do no harm. There is no one to worry over, to wonder if this will be seen as morbid, a sticky fascination with death. But this is my gift to you. It may be unnecessary. I think of you as a blank slate, but then again, you may know much more than I do. Humor me, then, little one.

The slope we all descend is riddled with holes, exits. Some of us, mostly due to circumstances we don't control but proudly take credit for, avoid the holes for many years. Others, for reasons also beyond control, fall through early. No matter when it happens the rest of us are shocked. Call it love of life. Call it denial. We keep moving, dodging holes whether we realize it or not. Some of us walk with eyes up; some of us chose each step with our face to the ground. It doesn't matter. In the end you fall through. Then you wait for someone to catch you.

What did you do? I doubt that you can answer, but I still wonder. Did you *know*? Did you hear your mother's voice, soft like a murmur? Did you hear mine, not so much talking to you but there in the background, a familiar hum? When did you stop hearing?

She never told me for sure, but I think there came a time when she knew that you weren't with us anymore. She kept on, determined, chewing her lip, hoping. Praying. Maybe somehow you could sense that—her character, I mean—her farm-girl bullheadedness, her hand-to-the-plow-never-look-back striving. Maybe when she hiked her dress and clambered up a ladder, leaning back against the bulk of you suspended over the rungs, one hand holding her belly while the other scrubbed the walls of our new place, maybe then you sensed who she was. But no, I suppose you just floated, cushioned, and waited. The living always imagine an enwombed baby is always content, but I wonder. To be human seems to be always yearning. I know that we yearned for you. For years and years.

○

He forgot. Without intent, without trying not to, he lost whatever memory of her he had acquired. She became less than a shadow. Aside from the box of sympathy cards, there was no physical evidence of her existence. No fading snapshots to discover, no bronzed baby shoes to ponder. She was almost a legend.

Once he read a story about a family who lost a child to disease. The narrator was born after the death. She loved her dead brother, spoke of him by name. Strange, he thought.

Sometimes, if he heard of a baby dying, or a miscarriage, he would think of his sister. Try to associate grief with her. It was like staring down a deep dry well, like wishing on a dropped penny falling to the bottom. It seemed like the thing to do, but he had low expectations. Genuine grief can't be conjured. The artificial kind fails to satisfy.

○

We're taught that what matters is the space between. We breathe and then we live, we live and we matter, we die and fade away. The pat aphorisms are endless: Make the most of it. Live to the fullest. Make a difference. Seek God's will. Use your gifts. Live.

You mattered. You still matter. Why else would I think of you now, or search for you? But how does that fit into the economics of the living, the equation of life's worth? Your entire life contained in the womb, suspended in potentiality. Then what?

We asked God, silently. We listened to words we didn't ask to hear. God's will. Divine Providence. Purposes. We stood straight and nodded acceptance. And buried you. A seed, the Bible says.

You fell through and someone reached out and caught you.

○

He thinks he's fabricated the memory. The car may be real and his mother's scarf and surely her pinched smile. But the rest, he decides, is imagined. Murky truth. The grass seems right, in need of cutting, and the place is flat and close to the road. There are others, though, kneeling, and he is there too. Standing back a bit and looking down at a small bronze plaque. Name, date, letters raised and Roman. Baby Land. Later, he will snort at that name, but now he is silent. Sister, he thinks. Strange.

○

I am falling, too, waiting to be caught. I wonder if I will find you and how I will know you are you. Will you know me? Will we have a family reunion of sorts, a gathering of my parents and brothers and the others who, like you, died before I knew them? Are you still flesh of my flesh?

I never saw you. Instead, I went to your mother. I should have, but I should have gone to you, too. Held you —at least with my eyes. I would have *known* you, just for a moment. Maybe that would have been enough.

Instead, I *arranged*. I called family. I bought a funeral plot—three-hundred-seventy-five dollars—in a sad corner of the cemetery where the newborns lay in narrow rows under miniature markers. I bought a marker, too. Paid for it with installments. I made all these decisions and barely consulted your mother, barely considered her. When Sunday came and your mother was released, I sat your sisters down and asked for their help. I knew it would be hard, wheeled out in that parade of mothers and babies, her lap empty. They looked at me with big earnest eyes, solemn hands folded, and nodded. They did it, too. Greeted their mother—your mother—with smiles and hugs. Surrounded her. We went home without you, with just a fierce ache where you had been.

We went on. Back then miscarriages and stillbirths were more common. Today we mourn differently, openly, but maybe too sentimentally. Funerals shouldn't be a party. Hope of resurrection and all considered, life remains essentially good. Death remains a paradox of delivery and defeat. For now, at least.

But for you, little one, death was a very peculiar thing. The life you lost—well I can't explain my bewilderment. I mourned your loss as much as ours. Stillborn. Forever still.

○

He is a replacement. Born thirteen months after his sister was buried. It takes the vantage point of middle-age to appreciate the chronology. So like her to plunge ahead, mask emotion, set her face forward. He is born a balm for an open wound, a tattoo to transform scars. Flooded with unspent love and attention. Watched over until he chafes.

○

The incline dragged us forward. Not to forget you, little one, or to intentionally leave you behind, but because life insists on movement. Your sisters demanded it, pulsing with flesh and blood, racing from adventure to adventure. Their smiles didn't bend under the weight of you. You shouldn't feel the need to forgive them. They didn't forget you; they simply didn't know you. They missed what they could. They missed the thought of you, the promise of your arrival, the anticipation. They could hardly miss *you*.

We missed you. I'm certain. We tried to keep you with us, to conserve you, but life refuses to drag the dead along.

Memories can be carried, slipped into pockets, packed into stories, but the remembered remain behind, fading in long and graying shadows. Every so often, we stopped and looked back, and I know now that what we saw was memory, a moment, a place. You were never under that bronze plaque. You weren't in the knit cap you never wore. Even the loss, written in cards and wrapped in stiff and sympathetic embrace, was not you. You were only real inside her, entombed in flesh. Flesh going the way of all flesh.

Now you and I have more in common—not only shared genetic code, or culture or tradition—but common condition. I'm already a memory, shaped and stored in stories. The farther removed in time, the more I become a question. It's not quite the same, I know. Your story was so short it requires little more than a period for punctuation. Mine, for now, is told in chapters, with well-formed sentences, even footnotes here and there. For the most part it will be true, if not accurate. But wait. Time erodes. Details fall away, names and dates and places become questions to puzzle over. Whole chapters disappear. Finally, I too will be a name on a marker, a census statistic, a shadowy ancestor. We will become, in the eyes of mortals, equally insignificant.

Perhaps by then I will have found you.

○

He returns without having planned to. Work brings him a mile or two from the cemetery and something, the rolling land or a smell or the bend of the light through the windshield, reminds him. He drives slowly through town.

Five decades have transformed it from a village in its own right to another sprawled suburban shopping district. The cemetery has grown up, too, with trees old enough to be dying, drives paved with cracked and gray asphalt, signs that lean on bent posts.

He turns right at the first fork, somehow knowing the way to Baby Land. He parks on the grass and walks across the clovered-turf, down a gentle slope, to where he can just make out rows of flat, weathered slabs not much larger than paving bricks. He wanders left and right, reading names and dates, the words as brief as infant lifespans. He works toward the road where the lawn stops against a cattail-choked ditch.

Her marker is two rows from the road. He snaps a picture with his phone. Then he squats and brushes aside dead grass clippings. Cars rushing beyond the cattails raise a hot asphalt breeze. In a nearby field a clanking bulldozer pushes topsoil into large piles.

He stays for only a moment. His father is buried there, too, in an expanse of flat grass called the Garden of the Gospels. It is hard to find his marker. He stands briefly there, snaps another photo. His mother's side of the plaque waits to be completed. Someday they'll bring in a backhoe, lever the marker aside, dig another hole. He assures himself that will be the next time he returns, then walks away, listening to the dry grass crunch under his feet.

○

My body, or what is left of it, lies a few hundred feet from yours. I suppose your mother has been by the graveside a time or two. Your siblings, I suspect, are less sentimental, at least about final resting places. When the kids were growing we visited your grave a few times, but I never made it a ritual. Not because it opened wounds— they opened easily enough without my carrying flowers to them. As much as I appreciate the biblical imagery of a seed planted, I never felt you were there. In my mind of faith and my heart of love, you were already gone. Gone on ahead.

Unlike you, I was sick for several months, fighting as long as I could, digging in my heels until the last few days. I've said it more than once—God is good, and life is, too. Yours, little one, no matter how brief, was a life. Our mourning confirmed its worth.

So, I wait. Wait to come to rest, wait to find you and know you, wait to live this new and promised life that, in a few dark moments, I sometimes doubted. Doubt is something I know you never suffered. You never stood at a graveside, never read the relentless news of war and hate, never felt the shame of your own sin or the hurt caused by someone you love. Incapable of doubt, I wonder if you are capable of belief. Do you hope that someday you will rise? No, I suppose you don't need to believe. You just know.

Pretty Black Girl

This is what they did that summer. They stood tall and stubborn in the lake and let the waves hammer against them. They knelt at the beach and dug; dragging armloads of wet sand into walls and watchtowers encircled by ever-eroding moats. They ran the dunes, dull knives of dune grass flailing their sandy legs. They hid out of the wind and listened—to the sand shift, the gulls croak like old men, the lake lift and fall and lift and fall until the sun burst and spread and sank somewhere far beyond Milwaukee.

The two of them alone, stuck between the older kids who played endless games of volleyball, and the little ones whose inflatable swimmies puffed their arms. In the morning they followed the plank trail that angled between the cottages, boards cool and gritty on their feet. Old couples walked the edge of the water hand-in-hand, white shoes scuffing noisily across the packed sand. Once, climbing a dune, they looked down into a hollow and spotted a boy and girl sleeping, entwined under a blanket. Empty beer cans formed a half-circle around them. The girl's sun-burned shoulder and arm exposed to their stares. For many mornings after that they left the path and climbed dunes, eager for more discoveries.

In the first week of August, Adam—the tall one, the bold one—found a half empty pack of Marlboros. He tucked this treasure inside the waist band of his shorts. Stopping in the shadow of the beach house, they smelled the contents. Adam tapped out a bent cigarette and fitted it reverently between fingers, clamping it in his lips. He leaned toward Chuck, who cupped his hands around an imaginary flame. They laughed like children posing in grown-up shoes. The boys began walking without apparent destination, skittering pebbles with bare feet, slipping through back parking lots, stopping to toss stones at a corked wine bottle floating in the channel. Finally, they arrived at the darkened door of the Driftwood Bar. Adam tugged the soiled aluminum handle and they slipped inside, holding their breath against the lurking scent of beach and fry oil, of smoke and the stale sweetness that they were too inexperienced to name. They blinked their way back to the bar and stood between cracked vinyl stools. There was no one there. The Eagles trickled from the ceiling speakers. Adam stretched across the bar and plucked a book of matches from a bowl next to the beer taps. He handed it to Chuck, slipped another in his pocket and marched for the door.

Purposeful now, Adam leading, Chuck a step behind, they ducked behind Van's Boat and Motor, weaving the rows of empty trailers and listing hulls, and turned down Oak Street. They stopped behind the old elementary building, its red brick face summer-silent. A playground waited behind the school, slides hot and mirrored in the sun. The boys dropped down in the sloping shade under the tallest slide. They sat cross-legged, facing each other. Adam tugged the Marlboros from his pocket and pursed a cigarette in his lips. Chuck struck a match. Adam grinned, leaned in and inhaled. With the first puff he choked a little, then leaned back and blew a long smoke stream out of the corner of his mouth. He forced smoke through his nostrils; he tipped his head back and formed lopsided smoke rings that lifted and flattened against the hot metal above their heads.

Chuck lit his own cigarette and together they smoked. When Chuck's was half gone, Adam flicked his own aside. He smiled, then swatted the cigarette from Chuck's mouth. He laughed and raced out from under the slide. Chuck watched him crumple the cigarette pack and toss it into the playground trash can. Adam ran up the shiny, slick slide, his feet hammering over Chuck's head. "Come on!" he yelled. "Let's go swimming."

Mostly, that summer, more than anything else, they swam. They chased each other through the tea-colored water. They kicked to the sandy bottom in search of stones and old bottles. They floated on the breath-like waves." When the current came from the north the water temperature rarely rose above seventy degrees. They stayed in until their lips blued and quivered, and then they raced for the beach and lay, baking in the sun, burying each other up to their necks in the sand. When the wind went the flies came, lighting on closed eyelids, biting at ankles, driving the boys back to the water. When the wind was strong the rangers raised a red flag that snapped and rattled. Mothers chased their children from the water while fathers stood, no deeper than their waists, and dared the current. Gulls hung in the air as if stuffed and suspended from wires.

Several yards from the beach a row of red and white buoys marked the limits of the swimming area. The older teens congregated there, treading water, bikinied girls climbing the backs of sandy-haired boys. They tossed footballs and Frisbees. Sometimes a couple would break from the group and swim to a distant buoy. They would float face-to face, kissing and laughing. Adam and Chuck watched all this from a respectful and awe-filled distance. Sometimes, unable to hold their elders in reverence any longer, they would gulp and dive and swim toward the older teens, testing how close they could come before they were seen. Even though there was no place to hide in the water, the older kids never seemed to notice.

Halfway between the shoreline and the parking lot the beach house spread across an expanse of sand-swept concrete. It was really two low-slung buildings of yellow brick, connected in the middle by an open A-frame roof. One building contained restrooms and showers. The other housed the park office and the beach store, where tanned, unsmiling girls sold hot dogs and cheap paper kites and, for the sun-beat, aspirin in foil envelopes. The buildings stank of wet diapers, spilled ice cream and suntan lotion. Bees hovered over the trash cans. The boys avoided the place, tiptoeing the damp concrete only when they had to pee.

On busy days people stood in long, wiggling lines waiting for the toilets. Writhing little boys tugged on their fathers' hands. Inside the rusting steel doors the line snaked across the tile floor, always cold, always wet. Toilets overflowed. Faucets trickled, but failed to turn off. Naked men showered sand from their sunburned skin and talked Tiger baseball. Older boys discussed girls. Adam and Chuck lingered, listened, acquired a new vocabulary. Then they would walk the beach silently, sneaking looks, imagining. They scrupulously avoided eye contact. Sometimes, catching them staring, an older girl would smile. Most, though, stared back, blank eyes hidden behind oversized sunglasses.

The girls their own age ran in large, noisy packs. They stretched out on beach towels and rarely went in the water. They showed each other pages of glossy magazines. They sang along to top forty tunes on transistor radios. They rubbed baby oil on each others backs. They wore two-piece bathing suits that they'd sneaked from the house, daring things their fathers disapproved of. The boldest ones lay with the strings of their tops untied, just like the older girls. The boys sat in the sand at a safe distance and studied them.

It was Adam, though, who the girls talked to. His cocky grin, his shuck of black wavy hair among a sea of blondes, projected a jaunty image that he was inclined to encourage. A pattern emerged, scientifically certain. If he and Chuck hovered long enough, and the group of girls wasn't too large, maybe four or five, then eventually one or two girls would walk past. They rarely approached directly. It was usually the second or third pass before they would stop and ask something. Chuck observed all of this, first with wonder, then with envy. Sometimes the girls would invite them to move their towels together, other times they would all walk the beach, splashing each other at the water's edge. Adam never glanced back, never noticed that Chuck always walked a few steps behind, or that it was all about him.

When they were alone again, Chuck would try to force his way in. He grinned and snickered and tried a few of those secret words—*melons, jugs*—they had gleaned from the older boys. Adam would grin uncomfortably and change the subject. Chuck tried to follow Adam's lead, but instead, he felt guilty, dirty, then angry. At night in bed, he would confess his thoughts and then relive them. He would make promises to God he knew he would not keep.

He would dream hot dreams in which he knelt and packed sand over a girl's bikinied body, her face smiling as his hands shaped her contours.

Every Friday two black families came to the beach. Two mothers—sisters, the boys guessed—twin girls in diapers, a chubby boy of ten or so, and a girl about their own age. Adam said they sure were brave to come. They sure stood out. They arrived almost as early as the boys, set up chairs at water's edge and spent the day under two large umbrellas. The women read thick books and talked and tended the little ones. The boy wandered the beach in long trunks and a big t-shirt emblazoned with a Chicago Cubs logo, a declaration that set him apart as much as the color of his skin. The girl spread out on a towel away from the shadow of the umbrellas and oiled her skin to a deep polished bronze.

The boys discussed this mystery, pondering whether black skin could tan. They had never seen a black woman, or a girl for that matter, in a bathing suit. The women were attractive, but they were mothers and that made an unspoken difference to the boys. The girl, though, sometimes carried herself like a woman: her body loose and strong and her gaze steady when she needed it to be. They began to look forward to Fridays, when they would spend less time in the water and more time on the beach. They would spread their towels flat instead of leaving them in a heap. They pretended to read magazines and comic books. Chuck actually applied the suntan lotion his mother forced on him when he left the cottage and which, until now, he'd always stashed in the flower bed.

At noon the two women would brush off the little ones and unpack a picnic. They un-wrapped sandwiches, scooped potato salad onto paper plates and poured Kool-aid. The girl would come, but only after she was called a few times. Often the women sent her to find the chubby boy. Returning, she would sit a little apart and eat. Then she would pick up her small purse, slip her feet into flip flops, and walk to the beach store.

Each Friday, purse, then flip-flops, then slow fluid stride across the sand. Finally, the boys needed to know. They stood and followed. They watched from a distance as she stood in line for a large ice cream cone. She carried it to a shaded bench on the north side of the building. There she sat and looked out at the lake, twirling the cone against her lips. Even in the shade the ice cream melted fast and ran down her hand, dripping on the sand at her feet. She looked around, maybe a little put out for forgetting to grab some napkins. Adam tapped Chuck on the shoulder. "Let's go. Stop staring. Come on." Chuck shrugged and followed Adam back to the beach.

The following Friday, Chuck brought a sack lunch and money. When the girl finished her lunch and walked to the store, he followed. He managed to stand in line behind her. He smelled her suntan lotion. He felt the sun's heat radiating from her shoulders. He studied the faint texture of her skin. Up close it did not look like polished metal. Up close it looked like skin. When the girl stepped away, Chuck found himself staring into the flat chest of a tall, scowling blonde. He felt his face redden. He ordered a small vanilla cone and hurried away.

The next Friday Chuck waited for the mothers to call their children to lunch. Then he told Adam he was going to the bathroom. Adam shrugged and grinned. "Sure." He said. "See you later."

Chuck picked up his wallet. "You want anything from the store? Since I'm going that way? I might get a cone."

"Naw." Adam said.

Chuck waited under the A-frame pavilion, leaning against one of the stout, laminated beams that rose from the concrete in a bent and tapering angle and met its mate at the roof peak. He watched sparrows flit into the shadows, snatch bits of bread and chips, and fly away. A baby shrieked behind a restroom door.

He saw her coming a long way off. Except for her color, she seemed so ordinary, half stumbling in her flip-flops over the hot sand. Reaching the concrete, she scuffed sand from her feet and blinked in the shade. Standing there, her silhouette framed by light, Chuck studied the soft curves of her body. She glanced at Chuck, or maybe just the post he leaned against, and entered the store. She was already ordering when he stepped behind her. He had wanted to offer to buy her a cone, even order it for her, like something that would happen in a movie. But close to her, her tight dark curls inches from his face, he suddenly felt foolish. What could he say that would not sound stupid? He backed away. The counter girl handed over the cone and stared at the black girl in a manner both menacing and superior. Chuck couldn't see her face, but he was sure the black girl stared back, and for a minute he wondered if she would say something. Something harsh and loud, he hoped, because he suddenly realized he'd never heard her voice. Instead, the girl stood with her cone suspended over the counter, her eyes leveled at the other girl. "Thank you," she said. Drawn out. Polite as a paper cut. As she marched away the counter girl mouthed something and flashed her middle finger.

Chuck walked back to the beach. A yellow flag flapped lazily from the pole. Gulls drifted waist-high over the sand, calling taunts at each other until one would land and warily hop towards an untended blanket. The waves rolled with just a hint of white caps, and people stood in jagged rows in the water, jumping in the waves, laughing and splashing each other in the face. Adam's towel was abandoned. Under the rainbow umbrella one woman slept with a magazine draped over her face. The other mother stood knee-deep in the water, each hand grasping one of the twins. The chubby boy worked intently on a sprawling sandcastle.

Chuck thought about the counter girl's face and her obscene finger and the way the black girl—how he wished he knew her name—had answered her. He remembered talking about racism in social studies, his teacher showing them pictures of drinking fountains labeled *colored* and German shepherds straining at the ends of leashes, snarling at dark-suited black men. He remembered the riots when he was a little boy, seeing—simultaneously— state troopers blocking highway ramps and his father's troubled face. Still, he wasn't sure what he had just witnessed. It seemed too simple. Maybe it was. Maybe the counter girl was having a bad day.

The water rolled with white-foamed heads now and cheers rose and fell with the waves. Chuck looked up to see the mother scoop up the twins, one under each arm, and prop them on her hips. One of the little girls was crying, the other peeking around her mother's tummy at her sister. A large wave rolled and broke near the beach and swamped the boy's castle. He stood and watched as a large portion of his wall collapsed and sucked back into the lake. His expression didn't change until he turned and saw his bucket rolling among the waves. He called to the woman carrying the twins. She just shook her head and strained against the undertow.

Parents were lining the water's edge, calling and motioning for their kids to come in. Chuck saw a grown man stumble, fall, and disappear. A moment later he resurfaced, coughing, chest heaving. Except for a few kids still bobbing around a buoy, everyone was moving in. The boy stood still at the water line, watching his bucket roll in the crest of a large wave. It was only a few feet from shore. Chuck walked to the kid's side and said, "I've got it." Then he trotted into the waves.

He felt it immediately, the sand sucked from under his feet, the steady tugging of the current under the surface, the panicked sense that something was trying to drag him under. He stopped, located the bucket, and plowed ahead. The bucket appeared to stay in one place, but Chuck seemed stuck, too. He tried angling his path to break the current's grip. For a moment it worked. He dug his toes into the rippled lake bottom and took short, deliberate steps. The bucket surged ahead, away from shore, just as Chuck's feet gripped a wide sandbar. He splashed easily across the shallow, gaining on the toy. When he felt the water deepen, Chuck sucked in a big breath and dove.

He reached the bucket with a few easy strokes and turned back toward shore. The waves pushed forward, knocking him under water. He surfaced, scrambled to stand. His feet found the bottom. He lifted the bucket over his head in the direction of the two umbrellas, took one step, then two; then he was gone.

The water rolled him, dragged his shoulders down, his head scraping sand, turning him on his back. Chuck kicked and flailed and opened his eyes, searching for up. Everything swirling, sand and green and sun here and then gone and then here again. No sound, just a flat tumbling hum, his panicked lips clamped shut, his breath burning.

Suddenly a bump. Then light. Chuck felt the lake bottom scrape his back. He was back on the sandbar. He scrabbled, crablike, backward, turned on hands and knees, stood. A weaving chain of would-be rescuers, led by a tall man with a broad, hairy chest, struggled hand-in-hand toward him. Two people behind the leader, Adam looked up and grinned like a hero. Chuck accepted the man's hand and followed him toward shore.

When the water was knee deep, Adam broke rank and dashed clumsily, parallel to the shore. He scooped the blue bucket from the water and waited for Chuck. Offering the bucket, he wrapped his arm around Chuck's shoulder and said, "Holy shit! You scared me, Man." All Chuck wanted to do was shake his arm off, but instead he simply stiffened under it, and they walked side-by-side.

At the beach, Chuck handed the bucket to the boy, who stared at him without expression and then walked slowly to the umbrellas. The women thanked him, asked if he was all right, and told him he shouldn't have. It was only a toy. The twins sucked thumbs and stared at the rolling waves.

Adam plopped down in his towel and grinned. "What a day, huh?" He stretched out, hands behind his head, and laughed. "What were you thinking, anyway?" Chuck sat, shook his head to clear water from his ear. "You're back's kinda scraped up. You're not bleeding or anything, but it sure is red."

Chuck brushed sand from his legs and chest. He watched the women fold their umbrellas and stack gear into a red wagon. The girl stood slowly, shook out her towel, wrapped it around her waist like a skirt.

"Her name's Carly. Lives across town. Dad's a dentist, or something. Nice. Really nice. Not what you'd think." Chuck wanted to ask Adam what he meant by this last bit, but instead he asked, "How do you know?"

"Talked to her. Back at the beach house. I went looking for you. She was eating ice cream. She came up to me and started talking."

Of course she did. Chuck thought this over as the family finished packing their things and started the long labored walk that signals the end of a beach day. The girl Carly strolled to the water and stepped in until it lapped her ankles. Chuck liked the way her brown skin shone warm against the pale green water and fading horizon. When she turned, Adam called her name. She smiled lightly and waved. She walked with her sandals dangling from one hand and dropped on her knees in front of Adam.

"Nice meeting you."

Adam flashed his famous grin. "Yeah, nice meeting you, too. This is my friend, Chuck. He rescued your brother's bucket."

"Cousin." she corrected. "The fat kid's my cousin." Then, for the first time, she turned to Chuck and shrugged. "Kind of stupid, really. All that for a plastic toy." For the second time, the girl caused Chuck to flush.

"Well, it was pretty cool, anyway. Right, Man?" Adam laughed. Chuck stared over the girl's shoulder at the waves. "I'll walk with you." Carly shrugged and stood and Adam started off beside her. "You coming, Man?" he called.

Chuck sat and watched them walk easily beside each other. White sand clung to the back of Carly's legs and

Chuck absentmindedly brushed his calf. Adam said something funny and she laughed and punched his shoulder lightly. Chuck remembered the girl behind the counter, her hard stare, her anger, and for a second he thought he understood. He mouthed something ugly under his breath and—when he was sure no one was looking—raised his middle finger at his friend and the pretty black girl.

Altar

Go there in December, when barren trees frame the old house's shadow, their black branches veining the limestone sky into a cracked and monolithic slab. Winter, dull and gray-draped, seems to fit. No stray and resilient flowers to distract you, no green to shade a razor sharp sun. It will be cold, so you won't stay long, just long enough to get in, remember and get out, unencumbered by nostalgia. I'm not recommending it, mind you, but if you have to go, go in the winter.

Six winters I returned there, bouncing the frost-heaved pavement, slowing at the toppled gate, tires shattering the ice-glazed ruts. Each time it was bitingly cold. I parked a few irreverent feet from the steps and raced up them, shouldering through the peeling door without a thought for the dignity of the departed. They didn't notice. The front hall stood as empty as it did the last time I came, maybe the floor slanted a little more, tilting the entire structure inexhaustibly toward some central and predetermined point of collapse. As if some restrained but compelling force persuaded the supporting columns pillared in the dark and stonewalled cellar to rot. *So be it,* I thought, tromping my loud and dust-raising steps from one room to the next, confirming the absolute absence, the emptiness of every cobwebbed corner, the stripped-bare everything. Door jambs pocked with voided mortises where hinges once swung. Mold-blackened holes marking the location of leaking pipes gave the only sign of life. I marched a quick circle—kitchen, to dining room, to bathroom, to the larger of the two bedrooms where I had gambled everything away, and finally to the smaller one, the one we called the office. I paused, stared out the back window. The old willow tree scratched its brittle tentacles across the frozen ground. Spring was a long winter away.

If you go in the spring, it deceives you. Nature, ecstatic in her ignorance, hides behind jade-tinged hope. Stopped short by the jauntiness; the daffodils waving defiant yellow over last year's rotting remains, purple tulips perched on sturdy stems. And, for a time, it wins: life tramples decay, sprouting white then yellow then green. The earth-heavy air smells victorious, arrogant. By midsummer you might as well surrender before you go. The truth is filtered green by all the unrestrained showiness. You can get lost in it, standing in the curtained whispers of the willow, remembering things a certain way.

So you don't take my advice. Say you schedule your visit for summer. *So be it.* Let those leafy fingers caress you. Stand in their shelter. Realign memory. Imagine that old house like a thing of unblemished holiness. Just don't climb the steps. In the summer, the rain-rotted wood will cave beneath your feet. Save the ascent for winter, when the frozen fibers can bear your weight. And then, go only if you are strong, or if you have someone to go home to, to release you.

Go in February, after the fresh new year grows stale under the heavy skies. Slip out there unnoticed and stand on the rim of that blackened cellar, the remaining charred and crisscrossed beams dusted with granular snow. Once, coming back for what I swore would be the last time, I stood as best I could among the debris, staring up between the rafters. It was night. I watched the star-pierced sky until moonglow crowned the stone chimney. My breath clouded my face and escaped straight up into the windless night. Some unknown creature skittered its claws over the broken walls. In its wake the stones remained silent. The sky scrolled mute.

Leaving that place one last time, I drove fast. No more visits, no more sifting for answers among the rubble. Let it lie hidden until the day of all revelation. I slipped into my house, toed off my boots, pegged my wool coat to the wall. My hair crackled with static electricity as I pulled the knit cap from my head. My glasses fogged from the warmth. Then, tentative, unnecessarily shy, I sought her out, gliding on socked feet, peering around door frames, listening for the sound of her. She is always still, head bent purposeful over a jigsaw puzzle, or blanket-wrapped and reading. It is her eyes I need, and I wait—for the gentle tip of her head, the soft fall of her hair. I found her. Her eyes are hammers, blue-fired, and they knocked the brittleness from me. Potshards shattered. Freed, I joked and teased and played my games for her and she looked on, smiling and quizzical. But she knew. She knew even before I did.

There are no lies between us, only knowing without telling, healing without diagnosis.

The last time I returned, the puzzle was just a diversion. The house was warm with oven scent. The table spread, candle lit. I washed up and waited, restless as she finished fitting the pieces. She entered, elegant and restrained, her lips warm against mine, breath sweet with wine. She motioned for me to sit and began to serve our meal: bold leafy greens, crusty bread that crackled as she broke it. She poured wine, deep burgundy scents splashing velvet into the glasses. We murmured a prayer, shared words of holiness. *Now*, she said, lifting her glass, *To all that is pure and good*. She drank and I followed and then we ate, listening to the clink of silver on china, the sound of our breathing, the snap of flame over molten wax. Outside the night stalked. Painfully cold. Outside.

I cleaned up, washed the dishes and stared out the window, when I heard a door close and the car start. I grabbed a towel and walked to the front window, wiping suds from my hands, just in time to watch the taillights fade. I finished the chores, read, shuffled through a stack of old papers that needed filing. Finally, I went to our room, picked her dress off the floor and hung it, shut the half-open dresser drawers. I undressed and slid under a pile of blankets, shivering. The food and wine won, and against all my determination, I slept.

I woke to the impossible sound of rain, but it was the shower. She was in the shower. I smiled, groggy, thankful she was home. The clock read some unimaginable hour and I drifted off again, unaware as she slid in beside me. She was just there, her flesh goose-bumped against mine, her hair damp on my shoulder. She whispered something I didn't understand and then she pulled my face around and kissed me. I smelled her hair, a strange sachet of shampoo and wood smoke. Her hand, laid soft on my cheek, harbored the cleansing stench of kerosene.

Memory House

2:57 a.m. Matt sighed, swept the blankets aside, and swung his legs off the bed. Below him the furnace clicked and whooshed and he felt the first push of air rattle through the registers and sweep across his feet. He walked down the hall, through the kitchen, and turned right into the den. His worn leather chair faced the picture window. He sat, tugged an afghan over his legs. The window framed a charcoal landscape, gray on gray, the neighbor's snow-heaped roof soft against a faded flannel sky. Matt lifted his hand from his lap and reached forward until his fingers touched the cold glass. The sky hung so close, so tactile, that even as he let his arm fall, the idea lingered. Some things seem more possible at three in the morning than in the bright of day.

The window had been Anne's idea and he had fought it for some time. He was thankful that she finally won and grieved that she had to take ill before he saw the need for it. One stifling August day the boys came early, and together they pulled the overgrown bushes, pried away siding, and cut into the stubborn old house that seemed to stiffly resist their every move. He remembered the fevered tension between the boys, their soft curses, the underlying urgency that drove him to forget his own admonishments to work smart, use your head as much as your hands, and so on. He could still see Matt Jr. scowl at his ringing cell phone, answer with a gruff, "What?" and then suddenly soften and smile. Matt Jr. stomped the sawdust from his shoes and walked down the hall. A few moments later the plastic sheeting protecting the doorway had parted and Anne entered. Even the dust mask that her son had insisted she wear could not hide her triumphant grin. Anne held reign, her wheelchair her throne. He and the boys and even that old house with its odd corners and out-of-plumb studs seemed to straighten in her presence. At least that was how he remembered it.

They finished the project in three days. Anne showed her appreciation by spending hours in front of the window, alone or surrounded by her loyal subjects—from the squirmiest grandchild to her adult children—and Matt stood to the side and watched, until night fell and the room emptied to just the two of them.

Then the full assault, the clutter of disease, hospital bed, oxygen bottle, hospice nurse reading quietly in the corner, strangled breathing, circle of good-byes.

For a long time afterward, Matt quarantined that space, walked past with eyes and jaw set straight. Then a slight turn of the head, a step inside. Now it was becoming a kind place to sit and think and remember. It was here he started to build the memory house, on another sleepless night clotted with sorrow and worry. He worried about his mind. More specifically, he wondered if he was losing it. During the day Matt felt sharp as ever. In a roomful of his articulate and opinionated kids he was able to hold his own. At night, though, in a dark and empty bed, he searched frantically for names that could match faces—for dates, for details. He fought a restless, running battle. Fear and confidence, doubts and providence. He mouthed desperate, sweat-soaked prayers. Then, exhausted, determined, he began to test his memory, sweeping its corners for fragments, sorting, labeling and matching, and found that he knew more than he didn't know. Maybe, he thought, it was not so much failing circuitry; maybe it was simple neglect. Could he, with deliberate effort, recall what he'd lost?

In the beginning he worked haphazardly, his mind wandering down one track and then another. Slowly, over a month's worth of long nights, he crafted a pattern. Each night he would begin by remembering a person, or sometimes a place, and then move backward in time, assembling shared events and moments and people until the trail ran out. Then forward again, until he found a familiar setting or face, another contact point, and another dead end. Back and forward and back again until, sometimes exhausted, sometimes content, he fell asleep. In the morning, he would open his eyes to an empty house, to the familiar, insipid ache of his bones.

Over time the process involved more and more imagination. Not that Matt imagined memories; he tried to be careful of that. Instead, he constructed a place for his memories to meet. A big rambling house filled with long hallways and rooms. At its center was a dining room, and here, with generous hospitality, he seated his guests, arranging them in such a way that he could keep everyone straight. Details were as fluid as his memories, and the room shifted in time and place.

Sometimes the gathering place recalled the kitchen in his childhood home. He felt the spindled chair-back knobbed against his spine, tasted the meatloaf steaming on his plate. His father sat across the table, where he ordered the meal with a somber prayer at the beginning and would later end it with a long reading from the red-edged pages of the family Bible. His mother sat to Matt's left. She carried the conversation, asking questions and disclosing the latest this and that of the neighborhood. She passed the plates and encouraged second helpings, usually of vegetables. Behind her, Matt could see the living room through a large arched opening. There was the upright piano, its mahogany finish almost black with age, the heavy green davenport and above it a framed painting. The painting was of a hill topped by a chalky white farmhouse. It was more Andrew Wyeth than Norman Rockwell; more illumination than illustration. There were two large maples in the foreground and a weathered chicken coop in back, gray siding streaked with faded barn red. Matt pushed his chair back and walked to examine the painting. It looked familiar, a place he had once known down to the texture of the chicken coop's weathered wood. He studied it, until the breeze that teased the brush-stroked leaves swept his face. Then he stepped forward and climbed the hill.

Passing under the first tree, he sensed its years in the weight of its heavy limbs. Its shadow collapsed on him like a blanket. He walked past the house and behind the coop. The ground sloped away, the wind rippling tall field grass into khaki waves. He descended, his hands sweeping the grass as he walked. At the bottom of the hill, he stopped at a large dome-shaped stand of sumac. If he focused beyond the stand, the clump appeared singular, a mottled mass of green and brown and shy hints of crimson. But then, with just a shift of his eyes, he saw each individual leaflet mirrored by its opposite, each compound leaf radiating in undulating rings, each fuzzy cone, each berry. He bent and scooted on hands and knees under the leaves. Inside, it was dark and close and smelled of earth, cool and damp. He sat for a very long time, watching the light kaleidoscope through the leafy dome. Passing clouds closed the gaps in the leaves like shutters. When he heard his mother's voice, he was not sure if she called from the distant hill, or from the chair beside him.

And then he was back at the table. His mother was old and shrunken and the farmhouse was just a painting on the wall. And Matt, himself old, sat staring at the painting, at the clouds, that seemed to be moving.

If he could trace back to the beginning, to the foundations of the memory house, he would stop at that framed picture. But he had long since moved on, and while the dining room remained the center of things, it slipped in form and content to match the moment. Sometimes it stretched almost endlessly in his grandmother's basement, holiday decorations strung from pitch-stained beams, loud talk and laughter echoing off cinder block walls. But most often it looked like the room off his own den, a small space just large enough to seat those dearest to him. In his mind the room was empty but expectant, ready for guests. Seated at the head of the table, he would stand and wander down a hall, knocking, opening doors, calling his guests. Sometimes memories opened easily; sometimes they stuck, doors warped and swollen, the contents of the rooms kept secret. Occasionally an opened room would reveal objects instead of persons, and he would turn each one over, sorting and naming. Forgotten gifts, toys and tools. A book. His father's watch. Matt would line them up, in an order not necessarily chronological, but it a way that made sense, that held meaning. Finally, slipping back down the hall, he would look around the table, apologize for having momentarily disappeared, and greet his guests, remembering every name.

Anne was always present. He didn't notice her at first, maybe because she didn't fit into his earliest memories. Slowly though, the realization crept up on him that even when he sat, childlike, with his parents, she was there at the table. Whether she was child or adult was never clear but her presence was. When he asked her to explain, she just tipped her head and stared, as if the question merited no response. *Why not?* Her smiled asked. *I have shared most of your life. Why should I not share this too?*

During the day he ate at a table set for one, laundered only his clothes, stowed them in drawers beside others he dared not open. He drove warily, no one beside him to watch his speed, to warn him of changing traffic signals. During the day, he knew Anne was gone. When he slipped in to his bed he knew it, too. During the deep night, though, he woke suddenly sleepless and walked from room to room. The house creaked and sighed. Moonlight slit the blinds and clawed silvered shadows in the carpet. He moved as if the floor itself rose and fell, as if he tip-toed upon a somnolent giant, a living thing he was not ready to waken.

In the deep night the table was always set when he arrived. Sometimes Anne was already seated, sometimes he pulled out a chair and waited. She always came. Together they would decide who to see and then he would take her hand and pull her up. They would walk the halls together, knocking and calling out their invitation. For a time the others came, his parents or hers, their children, neighbors whose names he had long ago forgotten. But more and more he hoped the two of them would return alone. Anne shook her head. "This is wrong." She said. *You are wrong,* Matt thought, *It is not good for the man to be alone."* He could not say the words aloud. Instead, he watched silently as Anne shook her head again, then stood and walked down a long and dimly lit hall. He was not angry with her. She would be back tomorrow.

Matt sighed, shifted in the chair, rubbed the back of his neck. A shy hint of morning brightened the window. He stood, pulled the afghan over his shoulders, and slid his slippered feet to the kitchen. The doorbell rang. He glanced at the clock on the microwave, muttered *What kind of people ring doorbells at 7:17 in the morning?* and began a slow shuffle toward the door. It rang again as Matt squinted through the peephole.

"Matt! You there? It's Larry. Breakfast this morning, remember?" Larry's whiskered face looked huge and fish-eyed in the viewer. Matt flipped the locks and swung the door open.

"Morning."

"Good morning, Matt." Larry swung out his right hand. "I'm a little early. Looks like you slept in. I envy you, buddy. Go on. Get dressed. I'll wait here. We can still beat the rest of those old goats."

"All right" Matt said. He took Larry's outstretched hand and shook hard. He could feel Larry studying him as he returned down the hall. They all did it. Offering him rides, dropping by unannounced to carry his trash to the road. He accepted their kindness, even if he didn't necessarily appreciate it.

He dressed in *their* bathroom, raked his bristled gray hair into order, quickly brushed his teeth. He stared into the mirror. Such compressed space. Toilet, sink, shower. Drawers stuffed with lotions and soap, Q-tips, tampons, little shampoos plundered from some forgotten resort. The two of them jostling for space, flesh against flesh. The smells of sleep and soap and her hot curling iron against hair hung in the air, sacred as incense. Anne at the mirror, brush flashing, scowling at her reflection, turning shyly, smiling. He felt strong beside her, young even.

"Matt?" Larry's bellow bounced down the hall.

Matt closed his eyes, waiting. *Time to go,* she would have said, *Time to go sit with those old men and solve the world's problems.* Matt waited for the words, for the gentle push of her hand on his arm. He rallied his arguments: they never listened, he no longer cared much for politics, sports bored him, theology should not be a game. After all those years, he'd rather stay here with her. Somewhere down the hall Larry jiggled his keys. *After all those years?* Matt opened his eyes. They stared back, set deep in a face pale and cracked like old porcelain.

"You ready to go, old man?"

Matt stowed his toothbrush, wiped his hands, snapped off the light. His reflection faded to gray in the mirror. Larry started whistling a shrill and off-key marching song. *See you tonight?* Matt whispered. He did not wait for an answer. Instead, he stepped deliberately down the hall, where Larry stood with his hand on the doorknob. "Where's your coat, Matt? It's cold out there." Matt did not answer. "Matt. A coat, old buddy."

"Let me through, Larry."

"Alright." Larry shrugged and swung the door open. Matt stepped past. He stopped at the edge of the porch and looked out, arms crossed against the cold. His lawn looked tired, winter-weary, but there was a hint of spring in the dirty smudged snow. The sky clotted with gray, rolling clouds. Matt searched for blue. Enough breaks in the gloom and the crocuses would poke through, and then the tulips. It was too early, but Matt wouldn't try to cover them. *Let them rise*, he thought, *Like little shaking fists.*

He heard Larry drag the door shut behind him with a firm tug. "Door needs a little work, Matt. I can stop by next week, bring a few tools with me."

"I have tools." Matt said.

"Course you do."

"I can fix my own door."

"Course you can."

Matt stepped off the porch and walked to Larry's car. Seated and belted in, he studied the house as Larry backed down the driveway, put the car in drive and headed for the restaurant. Anne, Matt decided, would approve of the way he handled Larry, maybe even laugh. He would take a look at the door later. Probably just some loose screws. If it was more serious than that, he would discuss it with Anne tonight.

If I Had a Hammer

Every Sunday Ray watches the cars parade into East Presbyterian's parking lot. Usually he sits on the small screened porch, coffee propped on his knee. On hot mornings, like this one, Ray wears a threadbare T-shirt and gray boxers. He assures Grace that no one can see him through the screen. She smiles and shakes her head.

He knows the vehicles, their order of arrival. The old folks come first, parking near the doors and gripping the iron railing as they navigate the steps. The young families pull in next, assembling car seats and diaper bags, herding arm tugging toddlers through the door. Then Grace walks out on the porch and stops beside him. Often she brings him breakfast—toast topped with a shiny egg. Sometimes she just stands quietly until he turns. "I'm going now," she says, her small black purse tight against her trim waist. She still looks so good, Ray thinks. "Wish you'd come," she says. Ray nods and smiles. She leans down to kiss him.

"Maybe next week." Ray receives her kiss. He runs his big hand lightly around her back. "I'll make dinner." He watches her push the screen door open, descend the steps, and cross the street. She stops outside the heavy arched doors of the church and turns. He knows she can't see him, but she waves anyway. Then she swings the big door open and disappears.

When they first moved here, thirty-four years ago, Ray went with her, slipping into the back pew, standing and singing and always following Grace's lead. He shook hands and endured introductions, waiting while she made conversation, studying those strange people with their flat vowels and stern faces. Back then, it was a church of carpenters and tradesmen. New in town and out of work, Ray hedged about his past, unsure about their view of the long and now-ended war. Most listened without judgment. Some offered suggestions about who might be hiring.

A few days after that first visit, the black rotary phone on the wall of their tiny kitchen rang. Grace handed the receiver to Ray and rested her hand soft on his shoulder. Ray listened, said yes two or three times, stood, and hung the phone back in place. "One of the old men from the church." he said. "Asked me to help fix up a house for some Vietnamese refugees." Grace nodded. "No pay, mind you. All volunteer." She smiled and left the room. "Now don't go getting your hopes all up," he called after her. After a few minutes, he went to the garage. He shuffled through stacks of unpacked boxes until he found his carpenter belt. Saw dust sifted from the empty nail pouches. The hammer still nested in its loop.

Ray worked alongside the men for two weeks. A big, balding carpenter ran things. Scowling, he handed out assignments, checked work, and coordinated everyone according to an unbendable schedule he stored in his head. His fading Semper Fi tattoo left Ray wondering. Ray watched the church folks, skilled and otherwise, patch walls and hang doors, scrub sinks and update wiring. Each night the house crowded with volunteers, so many that the hallways clogged like stopped drain pipes. Eager parents equipped their children with scrub brushes and brooms.

Once Ray watched a mother slap her teenage son's face so hard that he winced. Just before, Ray heard the boy mutter something about cleaning a house for a bunch of gooks.

One evening the father of the refugee family toured the house. The big carpenter and a translator led him around; he smiled and bowed, somehow standing proud among all those towering Dutch folk. Ray retreated to the backyard. Shaking, he lit a cigarette and squatted, squinting at the house. His right hand formed a fist. He forced it open and pressed it flat against his leg.

Over the next six years, three families occupied the house, found jobs, acquired a rudimental but sufficient English, and moved on. They politely attended services with their sponsors and then slowly, almost carefully returned to their own religious affiliations. They were Catholics and Buddhists and unbelievers. Ray found permanent work with the big carpenter. A refugee himself, Ray hung at the edges of the church. Then, like the smiling people with their strange customs, he quietly drifted away.

Ray waits until he hears music carry from the church. He listens, then rises and carries his cup to the kitchen. He tugs on a pair of battered jeans and strolls through the porch and down the steps. The Sunday paper lays rolled in its plastic skin, limp on the sun-stained grass. He peels it free and sits, separating colorful ads from black and white news into two piles at his feet. The front page is cluttered with war and rumors of more. Promises of troop withdrawal. Warnings of new conflicts. He snorts, shaking his head at the U.N.'s strongly-worded warning to Syria. Locally, the city police declare war on street gangs. On the opinion page, pundits argue the wisdom of arming school teachers. Suddenly full, Ray ignores the other pile and tosses the paper through the screen door. The music from the church stops and Ray pictures the preacher reading the scripture before the sermon. Above, the sun nears its peak in the steel blue sky. He begins to walk.

Two blocks from their house, a two-story building stands surrounded by scaffolding. Ray stops to watch a crew of volunteers, dark-haired men, some bearded, scrabbling up ladders, mixing mortar, passing concrete blocks from gloved hand to gloved hand. Cars crowd the dusty lot. Not a pickup truck in sight. Ray has marked their progress for months. The building sat quiet for weeks at a time, then burst upward in spasms. A painted plywood sign displays the finished building. Its strange characters are probably Arabic, but to Ray they may as well be Vietnamese. Grace has often mentioned the church's puzzlement over this new neighbor. They've held prayer meetings and invited experts on Islam to enlighten them. Finally, Grace and a few others formed a welcoming delegation. "Well?" Ray asked when she returned, "Did you build any bridges?" Grace shrugged. "Build?" She said, "No, but maybe we chipped away at some walls."

A group of men assembles around a bunk of two-by-fours. They begin carrying stacks of lumber through the arched opening that will be the front door. Ray listens as a saw whines. The familiar clatter of cut-offs hitting the floor. Then the competent rhythm of hammer blows. They're doing all right, Ray thinks. He stands in the shade of a big maple and watches, patting his pockets for a phantom pack of cigarettes. He quit years ago, but the memories die hard.

Ray crosses the street and wanders back. When the first tower came down, he was at work, arguing with a plumber about the clumsy holes he'd just drilled through a joist. The news from New York trickled from the painter's radio, but they were too busy to understand. Planes crashing into skyscrapers. Somewhere else. Some other New York nonsense. But, as the enormity descended the saws and nailers quieted and one by one, they all gathered around the paint-splattered radio and listened, cursing softly, glancing at the sky. Some broke the circle, sat in their trucks and called their wives. Finally, Ray sent everyone home.

Ray stops just short of the church. The last time he went inside, except to complete some repair Grace volunteered him for, was the night of September 11. People arrived throughout the afternoon, bewildered, desperate for each other. The pastor opened the doors, and by 7:00 p.m. a packed church gathered for prayer. Ray walked beside Grace through those big, sun-grayed doors and stood with head bowed. The organ was silent. Listening to the shuffle of feet across the carpet, Ray heard the sound of boots, the soft rattle of gear. Grace wept. The pastor prayed mercy on an unknown enemy and comfort for all. Grace reminded him of that later, when the nation roiled for vengeance and the machines of war clattered. Ray shrugged. "Sure," he whispered, "but did anyone listen?"

The music begins again, a triumphant hymn sending them out. Ray crosses the street, angling toward the house. Inside, he fixes a light lunch, eats his portion, and leaves Grace's in the fridge. Then he laces his work boots.

When Grace steps outside, she sees Ray—carpenter's bag slung from his shoulder, hammer swinging—walking toward the mosque.

DNA

"It's the DNA, man. You know that? The D.N. A. You know what that shit is, right?"

I nod my answer, but his eyes stare down into his mug. He pinches the little red straw between finger and thumb, spinning a caffeinated whirlpool. With the other hand he taps a torn bag of sugar on the mug's lip, emptying its contents in measured jerks. When he's finished, he crumples the bag and grabs another from the stack at his elbow. The freed stir-straw propellers in the current.

"I mean everything! Eye color, shape of your nose, whether you're gonna go cue ball bald by forty-three. But big shit too! Brain power. Coordination. Artistic ability. Alcoholism. Allergies." Finally he looks up, eyes glinted chromium. "How well you can please the ladies." He laughs; a shaking, down-in-the-throat clatter that stops and starts without build up or fade. Too late, I catch myself grinning. He smirks and wags his nicotined finger inches from my chest.

"Liked that one did you?" I don't need to respond. He is already glancing around, patting his pockets. "Damn! Used to could smoke in here. Shit, it's cold outside. Not everyone gets cancer ya know. It's in the genes, man, everything's in the genes and the damn DNA. Betcha know someone who smoked into their nineties. Your great-grandpa or somethin'. Still, mostly it gets ya. Mostly it does." He stops and takes a sip of his coffee, smacks his lips, smiles. "But, coffee! That shit's good for you. If it has enough sugar in it." He rocks his head back and laughs. I grab the pile of wadded sugar packets and head back to the kitchen for more. Behind the counter the other volunteers huddle by the ancient fridge, their conversation harmonizing with its gasping compressor. After distributing the night's supply of free food, their duties are reduced to pouring coffee and wiping the occasional spill. I grab a fistful of sugar packets and try to catch their eyes, to guilt a few of them out from the comfort of the kitchen. I'd like some reinforcements.

When I return Kenny is leaning forward, his puffy down coat swallowing half the table. The jacket fits him like cotton candy on a stick. His legs splay out from the table, a jumble of sharp angles and rods. One booted foot bounces to a frenetic beat. I slip a pile of sugar packets next to his mug and slide into my chair. Without looking, he scoops them up, divides them into roughly equal amounts, and deposits them into several coat pockets. "Thanks, man." He says.

We are silent, Kenny tapping his booted beat and staring into the coffee he seems to have lost all interest in drinking. I lean back, my eyes wandering the room. Only three other tables are occupied. In one corner, an intense game of cribbage continues to pull many of the regulars into a strangely vocal crowd of spectators. An empty table separates us from a circle of three women, one leading the others in a Bible study. *Yes Lord* and *Thank you Jesus* drift in soft echoes from their bowed heads. In another corner a young couple stretches across their small round table, kissing. I scan the large block-lettered sign listing the rules of conduct for Haven House. While fighting, profanity, shouting, alcohol and drugs are expressly banned, kissing seems to make the cut. I sigh, relieved none of us will have to cross the floor and tell them otherwise.

"I used to think it was the blood. That's what my dad told me." Kenny's voice sinks into mimicked baritone. "'It's in your blood, Son. It's all about the blood.'" His father's words remind me of an old song I can't quite place. "I never bought it. If it's true, then bleed me out, man. Tap me dry and pump me full of better stuff." Kenny sits up and rakes both hands through his long, butter blonde hair, pushing it back from his face. He squints at me, tiny wrinkled rays fanning from the corner of his eyes. "My dad said that wouldn't work, they couldn't get it all out and the new stuff—the good stuff—would just get contaminated. New wine in old wine skins, and all that. But I didn't buy it. Even *some* good blood would be better than the sewer slop running through my veins."

I want to respond, offer something wise and comforting, something as true and ancient as the doctrine of original sin, but maybe updated. Instead, I sit and do my best to look him in his smoky green eyes.

"But it ain't the blood. It's deeper than that. So, my old man was wrong, but he was right, too." Kenny laughs. "DNA is in everything. Every cell. Every chromosome. Try to drain that stuff out of you."

"Building blocks of life." I say.

"Building blocks of life, death and every screwed up minute in between." Kenny waves his arms in a wild embrace. "So, I guess I feel better knowing it. Can't drain it out, suck it out, burn it out. It is what it is. We are what we are."

"Kenny," I say, grasping my opening, "genetics play a big part in who we are, but there's more to it than that." I lean in, unsure where this will take me, but sure that if I'm going to say something it better be now. "There's your environment, choices. Choices people make for you, choices you make. Where you're born, what kind of home you grow up in, what kind of school you go to." Kenny sits up and smirks, poised for fighting.

"Nature. Nurture. Who wins, who loses? Toss a coin, man." He slouches, his coat sagging around him like ruffed feathers flattening. The group at the cribbage table roars and we both glance over there, distracted. I'm out of ideas. Kenny's winning and he knows it, even if he doesn't want to show it. For a moment I hope he'll decide to change the subject.

"You know what it stands for, right?"

"DNA? Yeah," I stall; I will never get this right. "De . . . oxy . . . ribonucleic acid!" My murmured attempt ends triumphant and I sit up a little straighter.

"Naw, that's what they want you to think. What it really stands for is, Damned Nature After all. All that nurture bullshit is just that. Trace it back far enough and it all comes down to Damned Nature After all. Your family background? Rich attracts rich. Smart attracts smart. Beauty attracts—well this one falls apart sometimes. Too often a gorgeous woman ends up with an ugly shit for a husband." He looks at me and smiles. "See, there's hope for you, man!" His laughter is short and fast. When his face collapses, back to serious, I look away. Over his shoulder, I watch the kissing couple pulling close over the table, their elbows propping their passion. She grips his collar with both hands. His hands lock behind her neck. Their hair melds together in a confusing cascade of black and blonde. I glance at the rules again, double-checking.

"But the thing is, nature ain't perfect. You know how it works, right? Simple really, crazy invisible twisted ladders of chemical information. You get me?"

"Not really a ladder," I interject, "A double helix."

"Wow!" He smirks. "B student in high school science, huh? You're smarter than you look. Like I said, sometimes nature screws up." There is no smile this time, and I'm unsure if Kenny is insulting me, or still on topic. I suspect both. "Anyway, I was kidding about the simple part. Believe me, I've studied it. Read everything I can find and holy shit can I find a lot to read on the subject. I know all about nucleosides and nucleotides, asymmetrical strands, sugar and phosphate bonds. I know about grooves and base pairings. Bases. Four of 'em: adenine, cytosine, thymine, and—damn it, don't tell me—guanine. Yeah, I see your eyes glazing over. I can't blame you. This isn't for the simple-minded. As much as I've studied, I can't explain it. You just have to get it, I guess." Suddenly, he laughs again. "You need the right DNA to understand DNA!" Kenny falls back in his chair and laughs so hard his eyes mist.

I've been volunteering at the Haven a few years now. I've completed the required training. I know what to expect. Still, this stuff, this really off-the-rocker behavior never gets to be totally okay with me. I try to laugh with Kenny, to share his joke, but he's taking it well beyond my capacity to play along. I look around the room. No one notices Kenny. The ladies are bent deep in prayer. One of them is crying, her shoulders rising and falling in gentle waves, the voices surrounding her soft like lapping water. Over in the corner the cribbage game pulses, spectators stand, leaning in, shouting encouragement that sounds more suited for a dog fight. The lovers stand too; they've abandoned their table, her hands planted firm and deep in his back pockets, his slipped high up under her shirt. I decide it is time to do something, rules or no rules.

"Parents. Family. What if I told you my father was a prophet of great consequence, that my mother was runner up to Mother Theresa in a holiest woman contest?" Kenny leans sideways into my line of sight. "Huh? Me, a product of good, upstanding Christians, seriously fine folks. I'm not shitting you. No dark secrets in the closet, no horror stories. My sibs are fine, excellent really. College grads, married, seven sweet kids who call me Uncle Ken. Jobs that pay the bills and contribute to the good of society." He turns and looks over his shoulder at the intertwined kids and snorts. "Relax, man. They're not there yet, still fully clothed. Bet he can't even figure out how to unhook her bra. Look at *me*. Explain *me*. You come down here, what, once a week or something and pretend you and me are the same. Like I'm not all fucked up. Explain that to me." Kenny continues to lean half off his chair, blocking my sight. I have no idea how he hangs there without falling. Finally, he shrugs and straightens himself. "It's the damn DNA. Nature screwed up. Some base pair got cross-wired and this is what you get. Crazy Kenny." He waves his hands along his frame. "Exhibit A, your honor." Then he sits tall, almost satisfied.

Behind Kenny, the couple leans tight in the shadows, the girl invisible, as if swallowed by the boy. I decide enough is enough. I start to stand and look back toward the kitchen, but Celia, the college intern on duty tonight, is already coming around the counter. She mouths, *I got it* at me and crosses the room, her spike heeled boots hammering a warning on the old wooden factory floor. Kenny and I watch her pass, her hips swaying with authority, and I imagine what's going through his mind. She stops behind the boy and taps his shoulder, twice, before he slowly pulls away and turns toward her.

We're still watching when the cribbage corner explodes. Shouted threats and scraping chairs and the slam of fists on the table—all of this jerks our attention just in time to see the cribbage board flying in our direction, little colored pegs trailing like a comet's tail. I duck, but the board hits the floor a good six feet in front of us. I look at Kenny and he is shaking his head, "DNA, man, whacked out DNA." I stand and start toward the corner, glancing at Celia, who is attempting to wiggle a cell phone from her hip pocket. "No, not the cops, Sweet Celia," Kenny says, "Not yet at least." He is already three steps in front of me and nimbly blocks my passage. I'm fine with that and stop in the middle of the floor to watch.

Kenny picks up the board and approaches the cribbage crowd, more casual than cautious. He slides almost unnoticed between three figures brandishing their fists and one guy fending them off with a chair. Kenny sets the board on the table, squares both to the wall and sits. "Who wants to play?" he asks. Nobody seems to hear. The fighters continue to circle. Kenny drones in a low flat monotone that seems directed only at the wall, but slowly one man lowers his fists and relaxes his stance. The chair wielder tosses a profanity but Kenny raises his hand, a wave meant to swat an invisible fly, and the other man shrugs and turns. He catches one of his buddies' arms and together they strut to the door. The third fighter waits, now it's clearly chair against fists and, after an appropriate pause, he leans in with one final shower of muttered threats. Then he saunters across the floor to the farthest table. Celia moves in his direction and sits. Later she will need to write something in the night's incident journal. The young lovers stand untangled, holding hands and whispering.

The chair man maintains his stance until Kenny finally looks up at him and laughs. "Put it down, man. You made your point." The man eases his chair to the floor and sits, staring at the empty cribbage board and then at the pegs scattered across the floor. I bend and begin to collect them. Gathering all I can find, I bring them to the table and pour them out of my hand. Kenny thanks me. The chair man is silent. I glance at the wall clock and begin to navigate the room, clearing tables of empty cups, sugar wrappers and coffee-stained napkins. Celia remains at the table near the exit, listening to the man vent. The couple leaves, in search of quieter, darker corners.

I stand in the kitchen, the staff cleaning around me without comment. The prayer group continues unfazed; I wonder if they even noticed the fight. Someone says "See ya next week," and the kitchen goes dark. Celia is standing now, gracefully guiding the would-be fighter out the door. At the exit she puts her hand on his shoulder, her face schoolteacher stern, and I imagine he's receiving a final warning about any future incidents, either here or on the streets. I wonder how that goes over.

With the last threat gone, Kenny pulls the chair man to his feet and walks him to the exit. He nods at me as he passes the darkened kitchen. "Nice work." I say. He smiles, stands tall, and waits while the other man gets his own dose of Celia's warnings.

"I told you man, it's in the blood. It's all about the blood." Kenny winks and joins the chair man, draping an arm over his squared shoulders until Celia wraps up her speech. Behind me I hear a muffled chorus of amens.

Chairs scrape the floor and the prayer group rises, gathers their things, and moves toward the stairs. They stand, waiting, until Kenny steps forward and says, "Follow me." Then he leads them out, boots clomping down the steps, his laughter rolling back up, an impenetrable verse, deep and clear and eloquent.

Good Friday

Carter and I argue a lot about music. Not politics. Definitely not sports. Just music; rock and blues and pop, if we are honest enough to call it that. Punk versus folk. Old guard versus new. Who's selling out. Why the radio plays such crap. It starts 6:00 a.m. every Monday. I'm still punching the clock and Carter's leaning against the wall, CD in his hand. "Listen to this." he demands. I shrug or mutter "Sure," and then toss it in my locker on top of a stack of old magazines. I don't forget it though. He won't let me. He'll remind me at lunch and then again at the end of our shift. Walking behind me, lighting up a smoke, tugging on my sleeve. "You've got it, right? Listen on the way home." I nod and shake off his grip and try to stay out of his smoke cloud. *Carter, Carter,* I think, *when are you going to let up?*

That's just the preamble, though, the opening shot, or —to use a metaphor Carter would like—the first chord. Tuesday morning he's straddling a chair in sight of the time clock, waiting, toe-tapping. I've learned to drag this out, to fumble around for my card, to slide it backwards through the reader. I act like I don't see him sitting there bouncing with anticipation. "Well?"

"Well, what?" I say, muffling my reply with a yawn. He just glares at me. "Don't worry. I listened. They're alright. Not my thing, but alright." I'm rarely enthusiastic, but I tell him straight if I hate something. Of course, that's rare, too. I don't hate much of what Carter feeds me.

Don't love most of it either. I consider it a fun game and play along. He's so passionate. So determined to convert me. "Carter," I sometimes tell him, "There's no right or wrong, man. It's just opinion. Yours. Mine. Or some overpaid reviewer at *Rolling Stone*."

"Wrong. It's doctrine. With a capital D," he replies, "The way of salvation." He's that serious. He always laughs, always makes a joke of it. But he never lets up. He's constantly slipping me mixtapes, or forcing me to take a listen in his van, trying, he says to drag me into the present. Move on. Enough of the Stones and Zeppelin, of those mighty sainted Beatles. "Johnny Cash is dead and Dylan is old enough to be *your* granddad." Carter emphasizes *your* as if to show he's so much younger than me. He tells me to let that old stuff go, appreciate it for what it is. History. The beginning. *In the beginning there was sound. And the music moved over the sound and separated it. And there was rhythm and melody on the first day.* And on and on he goes until music creates backbeat. Then, according to the exegesis of the learned Carter, all heaven came to earth, all the prophets, the priests, even The King. Still, he insists, quoting another fading prophet, rust never sleeps and rock and roll will never die, but it has to—it must—keep changing. *Hey, Hey. My, My.*

He's constantly handing me show flyers. Giving me tickets. Backstage passes. Like I would actually go back stage in some stinking little club and talk to the band. I don't even like standing *next* to the stage. Give me space, a nice dark corner to lean in. A vantage point free of sweaty bodies.

So last week he's at it again, ambushing me in the parking lot, shoving a neon orange paper through my window. "Go to this. It's an early show, a treat for the local scenies. Harder stuff, but I think you'll like it."

I recognized the band, a homegrown success story. I don't go to many shows anymore. My old crowd grew up and moved on. Occasionally I go alone, but it takes a lot to get me out.

When I got home I added the show bill to a leaning pile of unopened mail, magazines and yellowing newspapers—my "should do" pile—and forgot it.

I didn't think about it again until Friday night while I munched my take-out pizza and scanned the entertainment section of the paper. Towards the bottom, sandwiched between an ad for a tattoo shop and a used book store, was a tiny reproduction of the show flier Carter had given me. The word "TONIGHT!" in oversized cartoonish font perched on top of the ad, as effective as a flashing neon sign. I took another bite, readied to flip the page, paused and then reached for my phone. After three rings I heard Carter shout "Hey!" over a crush of background noise.

"Carter?" I shouted back, "Are you at the Amber Entombed show?"

"Where else would I be? Where are *you*?" His voice sounded flat and weak, smothered by the buzzing drone of a packed house. "Get your lazy anti-social ass down here. They're running a little late. Rock stars!" I could see Carter's sneering grin framed by his sketchy goatee. "Parking is gonna be a trip. The whole world must've decided to party downtown tonight!" That was it. The phone went dead against my ear.

It took twenty minutes to drive from my house to Division Ave and its two-block strip of bars and clubs. By a few minutes after 6:00 I had circled the block three times.

Fat rain drops smacked my windshield. I turned reluctantly down a side street hoping for an empty meter. Wind-tossed street lights winked on and cast swaying shadows across the dirty brick buildings hunching over the sidewalks. Cars clogged every space. Near the end of the block a slit between two buildings opened to a parking lot, where a handful of cars clustered in the farthest corner. I glanced around, expecting a "Private Property—Unauthorized Vehicles will be Towed" sign. I saw nothing but two rust-speckled yellow posts guarding the entrance. Just in case, I parked next to the other cars. Proximity suggested permission. The wind spat rain-dampened grit in my face and I ran with my eyes down, the rubber toes of my sneakers flashing like moon slivers in the murky light.

A small crowd of determined smokers milled around the club entrance and parted wordlessly as I approached. I pushed the door and felt it resist and then give as the mass of people on the other side shifted to allow room for one more. It was as dark inside as out, every surface painted black. A young woman, dressed to match the walls, smiled and readied an ink stamp as I handed her a ten-dollar bill. She marked my left hand. We exchanged thanks with a nod. It was too loud to talk. The room hummed with banter and laughter and intense conversation. Loudspeakers pulsed the final frenzied notes of some punk band I didn't recognize and then flowed into the primitive folk beat of Johnny Cash's *When the Man Comes Around.* No one seemed to notice. The stage, an afterthought in so many clubs, crouched in the rear, catty corner the door. An L-shaped bar filled the corner to my left. Between bar and stage people clotted around tall round tables and gestured with drink-clenched hands.

I moved in tentatively, angled shoulders wedging my way through the crowd. I searched for Carter, expecting to see his figure in the thick bunch crowding the bar, but I couldn't find him. I worked my way back towards the stage, looking for a spot close enough that I could see the band but far enough away from the inevitable craziness. Let them dance, mosh and sing along all they needed. I wanted to stand back and watch. The times I'd found myself in this circumstance before, I'd tried for a piece of wall a safe distance from one corner of the stage, but the stocky columns propping up the roof drew me to their base. I settled against one just as the band began hauling in their gear.

I watched, my back against the post, as the musicians and sound techs quickly assembled the drum kit, positioned amps and uncoiled cables. Their moves were well-rehearsed, rapid, guided by nodded heads and hand gestures. The background music edged back and the steady *brump, brump, brump* of the drummer's sound check came out like an invitation, drawing the crowd closer. Over-hyped fans cheered while the guitarists tuned, and dialed amp knobs, and muttered instructions to an invisible sound man. By the time the singer stepped to his mic and began to shout "*CHECK, CHECK, CHE-ECK*" with exaggerated enunciation, a crowd packed the space between my post and the stage. I watched it twitch, a dense mass of dark clothes and bright eyes and moving lips. It breathed out body heat and sweat, the sweet stink of tobacco and beer.

To my right, in the very front and center of the crowd, stood Carter. He bounced slightly, swiveled his head to speak to the person next to him and caught me in the corner of his eye. Grinning, he yelled my name and waved me forward. I just smiled, shook my head and braced myself firm against the column.

The band's front man leaned over the stage edge, one hand gripping the mic stand, and exchanged smiled greetings with fans pushed against the stage. The sound track stopped and the rest of the band members fussed with instruments and grinned easily into the dark. Murky ceiling lights flicked off and we stood in black, humming silence. First one guitar and then another began turning out high chiming notes that mixed in a tight, discordant exchange. The drummer tapped out a soft syncopation that traveled between snare and cymbals, added in bass drum as the bass guitarist joined. The crowd knew the song. It packed tighter, pulsing like a waking beast, a few hundred lungs breathing in and out as one. One guitar stopped, the other finished the measure and faded. The bass notes dropped off, cymbals chimed and stopped, only the snare drum snapped and rolled. Someone killed the last light and we stood in complete and waiting darkness. Nothing moved.

The stage exploded—one crushing burst of light and sound, full chords and angry cymbals, a torrent of shouted words. The crowd recoiled, then jerked forward, a breaking wave that shattered into a mass of pulsing bodies. Arms thrust upward, tattooed flesh tinted to the flashing reds, blues and purples of the stage lights. The last bar huggers set down their drinks and filled the space around me. Every so often the crowd would spit someone out, as if it had reached critical mass and could absorb no more. The discharged would stand panting and sweating, smiling a sated stare at the stage.

The band flung itself through three songs. Then it stopped. I guess you can only play so long before you need to wipe the sweat out of your eyes. The singer addressed the crowd while the others tuned guitars, adjusted amps and sucked long gulps from water bottles. At the back, the drummer repositioned his cymbal stands and waited. They were all drenched. The crowd disentangled and took a break, too, exchanged words with the singer, shouted song requests and generally caught its breath. Someone had dragged a round cocktail table next to me, establishing a way station of sorts. Its chipped white top was covered with smoking ashtrays and half empty pitchers of beer. People wandered over for a smoke or to rest their drinks. They barely noticed me in the shadows. They crushed out their cigarettes and scattered at the first tapped drumbeat. Smoke ribboned up and across my face. I didn't mind. The place was starting to smell like an overheated swamp. Somewhere, I thought, Carter is in his glory.

This time the band crashed through two more songs before stopping to deal with an erratic guitar. The crowd slackened, people took a minute to step outside for air or buy another drink. The table next to me didn't attract much attention. I stood alone, scanning the crowd for Carter.

"Lose someone?" I turned at the voice. She stood next to the table, a cigarette in one hand and a pitcher of beer in the other. Her hair was black and short, chopped in a ragged cut that hung over one eye. Her eyes were dark and lit and I wondered if she was into her second pitcher. She stood and let me look at her. I forgot her question.

"You're looking for someone." She pointed her pitcher in the direction of the crowd.

"A friend. His name's Carter."

"Sorry. Don't know him." She put the pitcher to her lips and drank. She didn't sip. I wondered where she put it all. "Sweet show." She smiled and tossed her head toward the stage. I nodded back. The guitarist had replaced the problem guitar and stood with his back to us, tuning. People trickled forward. The singer thanked everyone for their patience. The girl drew deep drags on her cigarette and then crushed it out. She set the beer down on the table.

"You going in?" she asked, pointing at the crowd. I shook my head. "Will you watch this for me? Go ahead and have some, I won't miss it." She laughed and didn't wait for an answer. I watched her bounce and wedge her way through the wall of people and disappear.

By now I was sure the place was in violation of fire marshal capacity regulations. During the break three huge shaved-headed guys wearing black tee shirts with SECURITY printed on the back shrugged their way to the foot of the stage and chatted with the band and the crowd. The lights dimmed. The music started. The throng convulsed in unison and the three toughs bobbed like anchored buoys.

The black-haired woman returned during the next break. Drenched, she walked like she had just run a 25K. She smiled and laughed, grabbing her sweating pitcher of room-temperature beer.

"You gotta go in there!" she shouted and then stood next to me, swaying a bit. I moved over so she could lean against the column and catch her breath. I glanced down at her now and then, but she kept her eyes forward, grabbing air in big gulps, nodding at people she knew. She tucked her damp hair behind her ear. Seven piercings dotted her skin. There might have been more, but I didn't want it to seem as if I was staring. Finally, she pushed away, turned and said, "Come on," and grabbed my hand. She was pretty and confident and I liked that, but I don't think I had any crazy ideas about it going anywhere. I just followed her in and began hurling myself towards the stage, waving my hands, trying to look like everyone else.

It took about a minute for the relentless motion of the throng to drag the girl away from me. Even if I could've followed, I don't know how long I would have stayed. I'm not a big fan of trading perspiration with strangers. Maybe I would've grown sick of it or literally sick for that matter, but I didn't have to decide. The music stopped and the lights went out and it took a confused second for everyone to realize this wasn't part of the song. A few people on the edges lost their balance and ended up on the floor, but mostly we were packed too tightly to fall. Instead we shuffled for space and laughed uncomfortably. The band's presence evaporated into black silence and we heard the storm outside tearing at the walls. Crushing thunder shook the building and the crowd jumped as one. Then, someone cursed loudly and we all laughed. People dug for cell phones until a pale blue-white glow rose over the crowd. We relaxed in the dim comfort of our technology.

Eventually one of the bouncers remembered the flashlight he carried for checking IDs and he clambered on stage. The band huddled around the drum kit. People began to talk, soft voices hoarse from shouting along with the music, laughter spreading like ripples from wall to wall. Finally the band reassembled at the stage edge. They sat with legs dangling, amplified instruments traded for acoustic guitars and an assortment of tambourines, shakers and sticks. The singer needed to shout to be heard.

"We're going to try a couple of new songs for you. They're kind of rough so bear with us. Feel free to leave if you want but it sounds scary out there." He went on for some time about how *cool* it was that people were hanging together through the storm and what a *sweet* picture of community we were all making. The usual indie-scene blather. I'd heard it all before. The crowd, however, quieted and hung on his words, nodding heads in agreement. When he finished a gentle applause pattered through the room. I looked around for Carter. Wondered what he thought about all this. I imagined him hiding a sneer behind his hand. He came for the music. For the experience. The rest I wasn't sure about.

The band managed a respectable go at the songs, but their power was gone, the vocals strained and tattered, the guitars frequently smothered by thunder peals. After the second song people began to drift away. Those who stayed tightened the circle around the stage. I didn't move in either direction and finally found myself standing alone. When they finished the last song the singer announced a break. I headed for the door.

Outside the air was storm-cooled and fresh. Rain pattered a gentle shower. I started jogging to my car. More storms hung to the west, thunder rumbled a distant threat and flickers of yellow cut like knife strokes through a tissue paper sky. Wind-driven litter chased beside me down the street. By the time I reached the parking lot where I'd left my car the rain was hammering again.

I slithered and stumbled through tight-packed rows of cars, their wet steel skins slippery as melting ice. When I finally found my car, my keys had disappeared. I patted every pocket, leaned over my windshield and tried to see inside, but everything was too wet and too dark. I slammed my fist hard on the hood and the SUV next to me squawked and flashed its headlights. I swore. In the crazy on-off-on light I could just make out the shadow of my keys hanging from the ignition. I ran for the nearest building canopy and stood shivering under it, rain drumming on the thin aluminum roof. I tried calling for help, scrolled through the contacts, shaking my head at my options. In the end I tapped Carter's name and hoped he was sober enough to help. Carter's recorded voice answered, *"Leave a message – maybe I'll call"* and I did, stammering a mashed up explanation of what I needed and where I was. Then I waited.

Rain sheeted off the canopy, a liquid curtain that walled me in on three sides, and streamed away in jagged black rivulets, coursing under shadowed cars, collecting candy wrappers and cigarette butts and dragging them toward some common destination. I remembered youth, remembered building dams in the spring-born streams that cut through the sand mine behind my childhood home. My friends and I spent hours armed with our fathers' shovels and hoes digging and heaving the water-weighted sand. Before the dam broke—it always broke—we'd catch our breath, while the muddy water rose silently, foam and sticks and dead insects caught in the slow circling current we determined to stop. We'd stand in the water until it lapped the top of our dam, until if we walked our wake would spill it over. Sometimes, one of us would reach out a finger and carve the slightest break. The water did the rest. It didn't need our help, but we liked to think we controlled it.

I felt a door push against my back. Turning, I saw light beam through the dark glass, coming from a flashlight pointed by an invisible figure on the other side.

The door opened an inch or two and a soft voice asked me if I wanted to come in. I shrugged and slid between the half open doors. The flashlight holder was a young kid, probably high school age, angular face peppered with acne, hair veiled his eyes. He stared at me, then stepped back, swung the flashlight to the floor and whispered, "Sorry!" He offered me a folded paper. I took it from him. With the flashlight pointed at the floor I couldn't read it. Muffled voices emerged from somewhere beyond my sight. Behind the kid a wide flight of four or five steps led to a large room. At the top of the steps a pair of emergency lights leaked half-hearted beams against the dark. I heard singing. I stepped closer to the kid. He flinched, then angled the flashlight beam so I could read. It was a church bulletin. Good Friday service. I looked at the kid and politely thanked him. I would rather have had a towel.

We stood there for a minute or two, the kid's face beading with sweat, mine soaked by the storm. Neither of us knew what to do. I considered leaving, but there was nowhere I wanted to go. The kid turned his head up the stairs and I saw a suit-clad figure start down with the premeditated steps of an old man. He extended a big hand to me and I shook it. It was meaty, solid and heavily calloused, a hand shaped by heavy work. He looked at the kid and then back at me. He pointed up the steps. We climbed the stairs together and I followed them to a pair of heavy wooden doors. They opened to a church sanctuary draped in darkness. Candle light flickered over a table at the base of the pulpit, dancing light off gleaming silver communion dishes. The congregation finished singing as I slipped into an empty back pew. The older man continued down the aisle. I didn't see the kid. I sat alone in the pew, which was fine with me.

Fabric rustled and a robed figure stood and approached the table. She stood behind it and looked out over the congregation. The usual murmur of a crowd—the scattered coughs and throat-clearings and whispered instructions from parent to child—softened and died. She began to read. I couldn't really hear the words, but I knew them as an echo. *Bread* and *wine* and *body broken* and *on-the-night-he-was-betrayed* triggered remembrances of mystery and monotony. The congregation began to recite and I watched four men stand and receive the offered trays from the woman. They slipped away from the table and spread through the aisles, passing the trays silently. The woman began to sing, her voice strong, the words floating over us without need of amplification. The song was unknown to me but the words were familiar and I closed my eyes to listen.

I felt a gentle tap on my shoulder. The old man was standing at the end of my pew, his arm extending the tray of bread to me. I began to shake my head. I heard the voices of the past—ominous warnings of eating and drinking judgment—but the man pushed the tray in front of me, his mouth smiled but his eyes commanded. I took a piece of bread.

The men returned to the front. The woman distributed gleaming trays of wine that the men carried with solemn steps. She sang another song. This time I didn't hesitate, but took the offered wine. I held the tiny glass between my thumb and forefinger and stared into the crimson-black liquid. The singing stopped. The room was as quiet as it was dark.

When the woman spoke, her words came as clear and sharp as the candle light. "Listen." I looked up from the cup. "Hear his words. Do this. Take. Eat. Remember and believe." I tasted the bread and tipped the tiny cup to my lips. The congregation stirred. I heard the clink of glass and the fidgeting of kids and, as the congregation began to recite a psalm, I slipped from my seat. The kid was sitting alone in the dark, an empty communion cup balanced on one knee, his hand tapping out a beat on the other. Thin white cords traced a path from each ear to his shirt pocket. He looked up and nodded as I passed.

Outside, the rain had slowed to a steady, warm sprinkle and I decide to walk back to the club, find Carter —or at least a bus schedule. I heard a shout and watched Carter stroll toward me from the direction of my car, a long thin piece of metal in his hand.

"Where the hell you been!" he grinned. "Call me all desperate for help and then disappear. What'd you do? Get converted?" He was as wet as I was and I wondered if I smelled as sour. He held up a flat metal bar with a hook ground in one end and scowled. "Couldn't get in. Not many cars I can't open. Sorry." I thanked him for trying. "No problem. Nothing better to do once we lost power. No music. Warm beer. No AC. The rain feels good."

We walked back to the club where Carter was parked. He lit a cigarette and slowed his pace to match mine. The heavy sky had broken up, fractured clouds, a few candled stars glossed the wet pavement. Carter chatted about the show and the party my call had saved him from. It was the usual Carter prattle—long on enthusiasm, short on content. I didn't listen much.

"Where were you anyway?" he asked.

"In the church. Out of the rain. Good Friday service."

"Good Friday, huh?" He held the cigarette out in front of us and considered it. "Maybe I should give up this stinking habit for Lent."

"A little late for that." I chuckled. "Easter is in two days." Carter seemed to toss that around for a while, then flicked the smoking butt into a puddle circling a clogged catch basin. It sputtered and floated in place. We watched it spin, and I silently rooted for it, willing it to resist the current. Finally it joined the rest of the circling debris, yielding to the slow relentless motion until it was finally sucked down. Gone forever.

"Late?" He said. "Shit, sounds like my timing is damn near perfect." He started off down the street at a brisk pace, on to the next thing. I glanced back at the church. People flowed out and across the parking lot to their cars, their conversations muffled by the trickle of water in the drain. Car doors slammed, engines started, the parking lot brightened with their collective light. I watched as they eased one by one to the street and dispersed, headlights arcing across the sidewalk and illuminating Carter's shadowed figure for just a moment as they passed him by, until they were nothing but fading tail lights in the distance. The street settled back to silence, water gurgled in the gutter at my feet, shadows slid back in place. I watched Carter's steady progress as he moved through darkness into the yellow glow of street lights and then back into gloom. When he made the street corner he stopped, illuminated by the sure light of the intersection. I set off at a trot, hoping to catch him before he slipped from sight.

www.ingramcontent.com/pod-product-compliance
Lightning Source LLC
Chambersburg PA
CBHW060226180626
46813CB00007B/2980